CHARISH REID

(Trust) Falling for You

A Team-Building Romance

Maybe your nemesis
isn't as bad as you think?

The supreme art of war is to subdue
the enemy without fighting.

-Sun Tzu

Contents

Acknowledgement

I'd like to thank the usual people...

My husband, Noah: for continuing to be my steady rock. When we complain about the present situation (and location) in one moment, only to imitate Richard Harris in the next, I know I've found my soulmate.

My friends: Sandy, Melissa, Katherine, Coco, Taj, Cass, and Denise. You've gotten me through this maddening year with weekly check-ins that have restored me. You've listened to the worries and you've read my work. Thank you for being present while I wring my hands in Sweden. You're all a different sort of soulmate.

My kinfolk: Aunt Carolyn, Sister Ronnie, Cousin Kristi. Thank you for urging me to continue. Thank you for reading and supporting my work. I hope I'm keeping the Reid name alive and well.

Chapter One (Day 1: Arrival)

G od, no, Peter…" Yolanda groaned. "Please don't tell another theology joke."

The back of the charter bus joined in her exasperation, but it was too late. Once Peter Leonard got started on his biblical stand up routine, it was difficult to stop him. "I see the English department doesn't have a sense of humor," he said. "Have you ever heard why Jesus didn't become a lawyer?"

Julia Crawford, her best friend from the History department, chimed in without even turning in her seat. "He got hung up on the boards."

Yolanda suppressed a giggle, knowing that Julia had suffered through most of these jokes because her office was right next to Peter's. After a well-rested summer, Yolanda could stomach Peter's corniness a little better than her friend. As she stared out of the bus window, she grew excited about the faculty retreat to the woods of Wisconsin. Their Humanities dean promised that the mandatory team-building trip would be a great opportunity to strengthen work-relationships and yada-yada, whatever. Yolanda hadn't fully listened to the year-end university meeting when Dean Craig introduced the idea to them. All she knew was that their private institution, Franklin U, had enough funds to send several departments to what amounted to a fun-filled adult summer camp.

Julia did not share her sentiments. With her slender arms crossed over her chest, she leaned closer to Yolanda and whispered, "You know I love you, but I also hate you right now."

Yolanda could guess why. She glanced at Julia's down-turned mouth and grinned. "You're still jealous that I get my own cabin for the week?" she goaded while nudging her friend. "I can't help it if Rhonda got sick and pulled out."

Julia sucked her teeth and made a face that didn't mar her pretty features. She was one of those people who still dressed up to go to the airport. A bus trip from Chicago to the middle of Wisconsin wouldn't catch her slipping. Her deep brown skin shone beautifully against her scarlet red maxi dress. Her lipstick was an impossible match and still lovely even as she scowled. "I'm stuck with Brenda from Communications," she whispered. "You know the only communications she traffics in is gossip. She's going to talk my ear off for six days. I don't know why I couldn't just bunk with you."

"They can't put the two Black professors together," Yolanda said. "It would look suspect."

"Fuck that," Julia muttered.

"How does Moses make his coffee?" Peter called out.

The whole bus shouted back in unison: "Hebrews it!"

That was their version of a bus sing-a-long. Yolanda was half listening to Julia snap at Peter, while the rest of her attention was on the man walking towards the back of the bus.

Her work-nemesis, Samuel Morris.

While everyone was gearing up for a loose week in the woods, History professor Samuel was wound tighter than a Swiss watch. The man looked like he was desperately holding himself together as he walked down the aisle, holding a package of disinfectant wipes. Yolanda fought to not roll her eyes. The rule-following, orderly, Dudley Do-Right couldn't stand to touch the common man's toilet stall on a bus, nor could he help himself from telling her to shush during all-campus meetings. If anyone was going to be a stick in the mud during this trip, it would be him. Yolanda had deemed Morris a nemesis because he had a perpetual stick up his ass and he won The Wilson-Kramer Grant that she applied for. That was a year ago. In the time she'd known him, they'd served on the same Assessment Committee, which was an autocratic nightmare with him at the helm.

"Hey, Sam," Julia said to her colleague as he tried to scoot down the narrow aisle. He stopped before her and Yolanda with a neutral expression on his handsome face. Yes, he was handsome. Yolanda couldn't deny that her nemesis was cute with a strong jaw that constantly clenched, full lips that rarely smiled, and a striking dark brow that always furrowed. "You excited for the team-building festivities?"

Samuel's forest-green eyes flitted to Yolanda before answering. "Hi Julia. Yolanda..." The terse smile he managed to eek out was pitiful. Yolanda gave him a two-finger salute and a nod. "Honestly, I would rather have this time to work on my syllabi."

Classic Professor Morris.

"Why don't you just use the same stuff as last semester?" Yolanda asked as lightly as she could. Even she knew it was too early in the trip to be spicy.

Samuel blinked as his gaze returned to her. His long brown lashes lowered slightly as he quietly regarded her. He inhaled deeply, expanding his barreled chest before answering. "A

3

syllabus should always be checked and rechecked before each semester."

Yolanda rolled her eyes that time.

But she cursed her bodily reaction when Samuel raked his fingers through his short brown hair. Even the small shock of gray at his temple added to his handsome features. And while everyone else dressed casually, he maintained his classroom look, complete with the white button-down shirt tucked into khaki pants. He rolled his sleeves to the elbow, revealing brawny forearms peppered with smooth dark hair. She'd seen his arms many times before this moment, but they still caught her off-guard every time. Yolanda squeezed the bottom of her seat and maintained eye contact with him, as if his masculine presence had no effect on her.

"If you'll excuse me," he said after a beat.

"Sure," Julia replied, settling back in her seat.

After he had passed them for the back of the bus, Yolanda exhaled. "That guy..." she muttered.

Julie's gaze slid towards her as her sly grin grew. "Yeah?"

"He just irritates me," Yolanda whispered. "While he checks and rechecks his shit, he makes the rest of us feel lazy."

"I finished my syllabi," her friend said. "Haven't you?"

No, she hadn't. Yolanda Watson worked on her own damn schedule. She would finish planning her English classes when she finished planning them... which was usually around the first week of classes. Sometimes students would get a complete syllabus a week in, and then they'd know what to expect from the rest of the semester. She'd had no complaints so far, and her student evaluations were stellar. As far as she was concerned, her teaching style made young people clamor for her classes. "I'll get to them when we get back," she muttered.

"Wait, do you seriously still hate Sam?" Julia asked.

"I don't hate him."

Her friend gave an impolite scoff. "You've had beef with this guy since he got that grant."

"The Wilson-Kramer Grant," Yolanda corrected. "And yes, those laptops would have offered first-generation students an opportunity to catch up with the rest of the Franklin U population. Reliable technology can make a huge difference when some of these kids write papers for me."

"I'm pretty sure that Samuel thought the same thing. Some of his students are *your* students, you know. You didn't lose out on that much."

Except she had. A year ago, she'd worked hard on her first grant, struggling with the wording and format. She was certain her ability to teach Composition would help her with the unfamiliar genre, but Samuel snatched it from under her nose. Not only that, but he was a prolific writer who consistently ended up in the faculty publications newsletter. His articles were always accepted into journals and she had even heard he was working on his second Vietnam War monograph. Did she have time to write? No, Yolanda focused on a positive classroom environment. She was busy mentoring students of color who were new to the college experience. Guys like Samuel didn't have to worry about that while they wrote about Hanoi.

Okay, maybe she was just jealous.

"Maybe you don't hate him," Julia murmured as she studied Yolanda's face.

"Mmh?"

"I know you," her friend said, wagging her finger. "You like a mystery. You want to know what makes a guy like him tick.

5

That's why you're interested in him."

Yolanda gave an indignant laugh. "Interested?"

"Yes, or else he wouldn't be living in your brain, rent-free," Julia said. "He's more interesting than the guys you find on Tinder and you know it."

The men she found on Tinder were…entertaining. Sometimes she found one suitable enough to fuck, but most of the time Yolanda had fun trolling them. Before she could open her mouth to object, Peter interrupted with another joke.

"What made the priest giggle?"

A collective groan came from those within sitting distance. "Mass hysteria," Julia said, closing her eyes. "Give it up, Peter."

* * *

"Yolanda Watson, English department?" called out their dean, Craig Kowalsky. He read from a clipboard while faculty gathered their baggage from the bus.

"Here," she said, hitching her backpack on her shoulder.

Craig was a tall and awkward man, in his early fifties, who always maintained a cheerful attitude about education. If any dean at Franklin University was going to start a team-building retreat, it would have been him. He adjusted his bucket hat over his bald head and glanced over his clipboard at her. "Gotcha! You'll be in Fox Cabin with…Rhonda Phillips, Philosophy department."

Yolanda nodded silently. There was no need to remind him that Rhonda was absent from the trip. She was this close to an empty cabin where she could go to bed whenever she wanted. The promise of walking around naked and snoring made her heart thrum with excitement.

"Mark Patterson, Theology department?"

Samuel Morris entered the tight circle of faculty members and spoke up. "Mark said he wouldn't make the trip because of illness. I was supposed to share a cabin with him."

Dean Kowalsky referred to his clipboard. "Okay, no worries, Sam! It looks like you'll be by yourself in Rabbit Cabin."

"Uh, actually," said a voice. Entering the group of Franklin University employees was a stout man in his sixties. His white beard hung to the center of his chest, covering the *Redstone Retreat* logo on his t-shirt. His skin was tanned and leathery, and his intense blue eyes scanned the group with curiosity. As they made room for him to enter the circle, he leaned on a tall walking stick and planted one fist on his hip. "Rabbit Cabin is in a bit of a state," he drawled. "We got a busted pipe yesterday, and it's gonna take a while to get that back on track."

"Okay then," Craig said, returning to his clipboard. "We're going to need to put Sam somewhere..."

Yolanda kept her mouth shut. Surely there was no way her dean would push for a co-ed cabin. But if they were really short on space for the next six nights, there was nothing to be done. Maybe they could find Samuel a tent...

"Yolanda's room is free," Julia announced.

She shot her friend a deadly glare.

Julia offered her a sweet smile. "Didn't you say that Rhonda had to pull out last minute? Whatever sickness is going around, Rhonda and Mark apparently got it."

Yolanda's heart sped up as she stared daggers at Julia. She was almost afraid to look at Samuel, who stood only a few feet away with his one suitcase. She didn't want him to see the irritation on her face. The thought of staying in a cabin with

7

her nemesis for longer than a night made her want to jump in the nearby Redstone Lake.

"Well, then that's what we'll do," their dean said with a triumphant grin. "Is that okay with you, Yolanda?"

Yolanda tore her eyes from her traitorous friend long enough to address her boss and the rest of the group who waited to get to their own cabins. "Sure," she mumbled. "If that's okay with Sam." She glanced at her new roommate and was relieved that he had the decency to blush.

Sam locked eyes with her and pursed his lips before shrugging. "Sure."

Their boss clapped his hands as if that was final. "Great. Everyone should go unpack, and we'll meet up in the main lodge in twenty minutes. How's that sound?"

As people wandered off to their respective cabins, Yolanda pulled her friend back. "I'm going to take you on one of those *Dateline* hikes and shove you off a cliff."

"Be sure to give Keith Morrison the photos from our trip to the Essence Festival. I looked really cute," Julia joked as she hitched the hem of her maxi dress from the dusty ground. "I'm giving you a chance to get over your ridiculous grudge with Sam. Five nights oughta do it, don't you think?"

"You're the worst," she said, watching Samuel walk off toward Fox Cabin. "And it's not even like that."

Julia pulled her arm out of Yolanda's grip to adjust her large floppy sunhat over her curls. "You call him your nemesis. Sounds like a grudge to me."

Yolanda had a hard time denying that. Every time she entered the same space as Samuel Morris, she had said something to that effect.

"Besides, I think you have a crush on him," her friend said

with a grin.

Yolanda was aghast. "What?"

"Try that shit on someone else, Yolanda. You're talking to me, and I know when you're thirsty." Together, they watched Samuel carry his bag in the distance. "Admit that you like looking at his khaki-covered ass as he walks away."

"His ass differs from the rest of him."

"The rest of him is pretty nice to look at."

"I haven't been looking," she lied. Samuel came to work every day in the same Clark Kent get-up: slim-fit khaki pants and dress shirts. The outfit was routine, but the way he wore it was hard to ignore. For a man in his late-thirties, he wasn't just holed up in his office writing. He had to be working out regularly.

Julia scoffed and rolled her eyes. "Well, he's been looking at you."

"Stop it."

"Girl, look at you. Even if the English department lets you dress like our students, you're still gorgeous. I've caught him checking out your ass too."

Yolanda's jaw dropped. "Are you kidding me?" The knowledge that tight-ass Morris checked her out was just as titillating as it was shocking. Most of the time, she showed up to class slightly late, wearing a hoodie and jeans. She told herself that she'd try to do better this fall semester. If she woke up early enough, she could work on something else besides her hair and makeup.

"Close your mouth, honey. You don't want to trap any of these country-ass flies."

"Just be ready for that hike, Jules," Yolanda muttered as she picked up her bags.

Julia draped an arm over her shoulder as they walked in the general direction of the cabins. "How long have we been friends?"

Yolanda laughed. "Long enough for people to suspect foul-play, I guess…"

"Sam's not as bad as you think," Julia said, hugging her. "I've worked with him long enough to know he's not very fun, but he's definitely not a meanie. If I can handle Brenda for the week, you can deal with him."

Right before they broke off into different directions, Yolanda smiled. "If I can't, I might try to make it work in Rabbit Cabin, busted pipes and all."

"Girl, bye," Julia said with a throaty chuckle.

Yolanda watched her friend walk towards Bear Cabin, leaving her to her fate of traveling in the opposite direction. She tried not to treat her path like a walk to the scaffold, but Samuel Morris was already claiming a bed in the cabin where she had expected to relax in solitude. No walking around naked now…

.

Chapter Two

S amuel tossed his bag on the queen-sized bed nearest to the bathroom and quietly appraised the space. Two beds, two chests of drawers, two nightstands with two lamps. No television, but that didn't matter. He had downloaded a few episodes of *House M.D.* on his laptop, but had plans to format an article, and finish up two syllabi this week. If he had trouble falling asleep, he'd let the wry-humored Dr. Gregory House lull him to deep slumber. Samuel had always felt a sense of ease when the sociopathic doctor solved tough medical cases after forty minutes of hand-wringing.

He'd need some sense of ease if he was going to share a cabin with Yolanda Watson for a week. He didn't *dislike* her... she just made him extremely anxious. She was a ball of loud chaos wrapped in a pretty package. When confronted by her presence, it was her beauty that made his speech measured, and sometimes stilted. She had a habit of arriving late for their committee meetings, wearing jeans and t-shirts that accentuated her curvy body. The top of Yolanda's head came to his chin, but Samuel wouldn't dare call her small. Her big personality and loud laughter also set his nerves on edge. People immediately forgave her tardiness when her smile lit the room. Not only did their colleagues love her, but their students sang her praises. "Professor Watson brought us donuts for finals week!"

Samuel had never had the desire to reward his students with sweet treats.

But he wished he could loosen up around them in the same way that came so naturally to educators like Yolanda. Samuel knew how to do two things: Teach American History and write. Every semester, he worked hard to contribute a chapter to an edited volume, publish an article, or attend a conference. Anything to prove to the administration that he could pull his weight. As soon as Craig hired him, he sought tenure with tunnel-vision. Job security after a hundred grand in student loan debt was a powerful motivator, but ensuring that he'd never be as poor as he was as a kid ultimately drove him.

Samuel had lived his life in a constant state of hyper-vigilance that made it difficult to form attachments to people. What if they pulled the rug out from under him and he was without a job, homeless, and had to return to Gary, Indiana the place he worked so hard to escape? That's why he kept his head down, proved himself at his university, and stayed on the straight and narrow.

But now, his peaceful week would be threatened by a woman he was certain didn't like him. Every time she saw him, Samuel could tell Yolanda was trying not to roll her eyes at his insistence on order.

While he stood in the middle of their small Fox Cabin, there was a knock at the door before it swung open. Yolanda stood at the threshold, wearing a pair of denim shorts rolled at the knee and a white t-shirt that read "I Fought The Law." She'd tied her voluminous black curls up with a red bandanna, as if she was ready for an outdoor adventure. "Hey," she said.

Samuel took a deep breath before speaking. "I already chose a bed."

Her frown told him he'd misspoken. "Okay?" She rolled her bag inside, made note of his claimed space, and tossed her stuff on the other bed.

"I drink a lot of water before I go to bed," he explained, as if it was necessary. "I go to the bathroom several times a night."

This didn't earn him a response.

He dug his hands in his pockets and walked to his side of the small room. "I suppose I should tell you now; I like to go to bed at ten pm. So if you don't mind turning off the light, that would be—"

Yolanda paused while unzipping one of her bags. "Excuse me?"

Another misstep. Samuel cleared his throat and tried again. "I'm just saying that I work better with a routine bedtime. And if you wouldn't mind indulging me, I'd really appreciate it."

Her large dark eyes swept over him in such a critical fashion, he was tempted to shut the fuck up. The imperious arch of her black brow made him both fearful and aroused. The way she twisted her full mouth and planted a fist on her curved hip, made him take another deep breath. Even irritated, Yolanda was still cute as hell. Was he allowed to think about his roommate like that? *Stay professional, Sam.* "I don't go to sleep earlier than one am." she said.

"Right…"

"Let's get this out of the way, Sam," she said as she returned to her suitcase. "I had expected to have a cabin to myself so I could let it all hang out in the Wisconsin woods. I have a backlog of terrible reality TV on my laptop I was going to watch until I fell asleep in the nude. But come to find out, there's a leaky pipe in the Rabbit Cabin, and I've now got a roommate. So, Rhonda is sick for nothing."

Samuel tried to digest everything she said, desperate not to get hung up on the part where she'd planned to be nude in the Fox Cabin, but what came out was nonsense. "Who's Rhonda?" he asked.

She sighed. "Philosophy department. Don't you know anyone outside of History?"

Honestly, he didn't.

"What I'm saying is, we're the oddballs who got stuck in a co-ed bunking situation," Yolanda continued. "I don't even know how Craig thought this was a good idea."

Samuel was also surprised how easily their boss paired them. "I assure you we can have boundaries, even in a space as small as this."

She paused from her messy unpacking and sighed. "You're right," she said. "It's just a week. We'll be fine."

He gave her a resolute nod. "We will."

But he could already tell by the way she unpacked that Yolanda Watson was a messy person. There was no system to the way she organized her bag; she balled her shirts and shorts up under textbooks and folders. In the meshed zip compartment of her bag, was a strip of gold-foiled packets... *Condoms?* Sam blushed and quickly averted his gaze to something on his side of the room. *What on earth did she expect to get up to this week?* Unless Yolanda was the kind of person who never unpacked her bags after a trip. A full unpacking was something Samuel did immediately after every conference.

She threw her unmentionables into the top drawer of her dresser and let the rest of her clothes idle on her bed. She hurried past him, into the bathroom where she spread her

14

hair and beauty products on every square-inch of their shared counter. He buried the urge to tell her how she could organize the various tubs of moisturizer into a better system. Perhaps he'd work on it when she left the cabin.

Once she exited the bathroom, she clasped her hands together and gave him a quick once-over. "Are you ready to go to the main lodge?"

"You want to walk together?" he asked.

Yolanda suddenly looked shy about the request and he felt foolish for asking the question. "We don't have to, I just thought—"

"—No, no, of course we can walk together," Samuel said, mentally cursing himself for sounding like a weirdo. He was only surprised because he got the sense that Yolanda didn't want to hang out with him any longer than necessary. "Yeah, let's get going."

He locked up behind them and followed her in the general direction of a larger building where their bus parked upon arrival. When Yolanda got to her group of friends, she immediately attached herself to them. His History colleague, Julia, wrapped an arm around her waist and pulled her close to whisper something in Yolanda's ear. Whatever it was, it made her hiss "Shut up." He couldn't help but think they were talking about him, but Samuel brushed it off.

As soon as they entered the main lodge, their dean and his secretary, Joanne Stuber, were at the front of a large hall standing before the dinner buffet. "Everyone take a seat and we'll get started," Craig announced. "Joanne and I are just gonna talk about what's expected from you all this week."

Yolanda and her friends claimed a table near the back. She turned to him and asked. "You wanna sit with us, bunk-mate?"

Samuel was surprised again. "Okay, yeah," he said. He chose the chair next to her, so she sat between him and Julia. Peter from Theology and Chris from Communications were also at the table. In his four years at Franklin University, he hadn't talked to the two men outside of university events. He'd at least been introduced to Peter's terrible Jesus jokes, but Samuel hadn't engaged in small talk.

The elderly man from the bus drop-off had also appeared at the front of the room. "I'm Gus Kelly and I'm supposed to welcome you to Redstone Retreat, so uh... welcome. I'm gonna give you all a run-down on the rules while you're here, so listen up." He ran his hand down his white beard and gave the room a once-over before continuing. "Safety is real important to me, and your dean assured me that none of you are gonna do anything stupid like walk off a mountain. Rule one, for the sake of fire safety, we ask that you do all your smoking in our designated area, off to the side of the main lodge. The Redstone employees will supervise all campfires and bonfires. Pick up your litter and don't leave food-stuff sitting outside of your cabins. You don't want the raccoons and bears pestering you."

Yolanda's eyes widened. "There are bears?"

"It's Wisconsin," Peter replied with a grin. "Of course there are bears."

She raised her hand as if she were in the classroom. "Excuse me, Gus?"

"Yes, ma'am?"

"How often do you get bears on the grounds?"

Old Gus chuckled. "If we're careful with our trash, we don't get that many black bears. Last one that wandered up here was two years ago, Ole Smokey, but I shooed him off without too much problem."

That answer obviously didn't satisfy her. She lowered her hand with a sigh.

"If you're planning on a hike, let folks know where you're going and stick to the designated trail markers. If you want to canoe or kayak the lake, see Martha at the boathouse for rentals and life vests. But based on the approved activities that your dean sent me, I don't anticipate much trouble outta y'all. I hope you have fun team-building and whatnot."

And with that, Gus Kelly took his leave.

"Alright guys and gals!" Joanne called out. "We're going to tell you about those exciting activities we've planned for the first annual 'Get Back to Humanities' team-building retreat!" She pumped her arms to hype the crowd, but they all quietly waited for more details about mandatory activities.

Julia rolled her eyes towards the direction of their group and sighed, "Jesus Christ."

Yolanda nudged her. "Shut up."

"The person you're bunking with is your 'TB Buddy,' and there's plenty of awesome stuff you're required to do together. Some of our 'TB Activities' will be TB Buddies only; these are exercises that you two will complete to better understand one another. The other TB Activities will be in larger groups, and I guarantee they will be exciting as heck!"

Julia groaned softly as she buried her face in her hands. "Fucking hell... TB Buddies?"

Sam could admit that TB-anything sounded ridiculous, but his anxiety ratcheted up to a nine at the thought of working one-on-one with his bunk-mate.

"I could think of a million things to call my buddy that had nothing to do with a lung disease," Chris muttered to the table. Yolanda gave a choked laugh that reverberated throughout the large space. Joanne paused her speech to look over at their table. Samuel held his breath as she moved on to the topic: a list of events for each day. He caught something about a scavenger hunt and a hike, but the people at his table were talking over Joanne.

"Guys," he whispered to the table. "Let's focus up."

Their talking halted with Peter shooting a glance at Julia before facing the front. Sam didn't enjoy being the taskmaster of the surrounding adults. If he had it in him, he'd laugh it up alongside them. But he wasn't socialized to have fun. Even when he was a child, he depended on order to guide him through a chaotic home life.

"So prepare yourselves for a fun-filled week of rollicking good fun!" Joanne shouted. She was met with the murmurs from skeptical academics.

"Rollicking?" Yolanda whispered.

"All right, guys!" Dean Craig jumped in. "Serve yourselves dinner provided by the Redstone Retreat. There are even vegetarian options for our rabbit lodgers!" He and Joanne doubled over in a shared laughter that made Samuel curious. *There's something going on there...* But he didn't have time to speculate about the dean and his secretary when the rest of his table rose for the buffet. Samuel followed them, hanging back as they lined up behind other colleagues.

"She didn't exactly say what we're going to do with our TB Buddies," Yolanda said, grabbing a plate from the stack. "Don't you want to know what we're going to do together, buddy?"

Samuel took a plate and some cutlery. "I guess Joanne wants to keep it a surprise?" Personally, he hated surprises. He would have appreciated a detailed itinerary.

"I love surprises," she said with an impish grin.

He figured. But the way she looked up at him... didn't make him anxious. Her grin made it seem like he was in on the joke, something Samuel hadn't been a part of in a long time. As he followed her through the buffet line, barely paying attention to what he spooned on his plate, he thought about their current situation. "I assume we're going to get a lot closer over the course of the week," he said absently.

Her surprised expression forced him to consider his words. He didn't mean *closer*, closer. "I meant that we'd gain a better understanding—"

"—Yeah," she interrupted. "I know what you're saying. Like, I'll know what your favorite color is or something."

"Right," he said, thankful for her save. He closed his eyes briefly and cursed himself for not thinking. "I'll learn about your leadership style."

Yolanda laughed. "Ugh, that's so boring. Wouldn't you rather know how I dress a hot dog. Am I a ketchup or a mustard girl? Do I like onions or relish?"

"How will that help our working relationship?"

She shrugged. "It's just more interesting."

When they arrived at the bread rolls, he chuckled.

"What's so funny?" she asked, looking up at him. Her dark brown eyes narrowed in suspicion as her eyes settled on his smile.

He stared at her for a few seconds. "You put everything on your hot dog."

Yolanda blinked. "How do you know?"

"Just a hunch."

Her face softened as she rolled her eyes. When she returned to the buffet line, Samuel realized that he was still smiling at her. He quickly trained his face to something more neutral and took his plate back to the table. He told himself that he was only making conversation. If he was going to spend the week with her, he might as well be pleasant about it.

* * *

Back in the privacy of Fox Cabin, Samuel willed his body to relax.

He was in his pajamas, back against his headboard, desperate to focus attention on his computer screen where an unfinished syllabus languished. But not more than four feet away, his TB Buddy laid in her own bed. Yolanda couldn't see his gaze flit to her every five minutes. If she had, it might have creeped her out. Which was why he needed to keep his eyes on his own screen.

But her throaty chuckle made him glance up again. She faced the opposite side of the room as she laid on her belly. Her bare feet swung back and forth in the air as she watched two women confronting each other on a reality-show. Yolanda had also changed into her sleep clothing, a pair of pink pinstripe shorts, and a tank top that read "FRANKLIN U" across her chest. His mind immediately went to her comment about sleeping in the nude. *Focus up, Sam.*

Awkwardness aside, Samuel continued to collect details about the woman who treated him warily. He noticed that she went to bed with her hair tied up in a large fluffy ponytail that she then wrapped in a black satin bonnet. Whatever her messy reality show was, Yolanda barely paid attention to it. Her focus was on her cellphone where she was busy swiping photos with her index finger. Samuel adjusted his glasses, which had

20

slid down his nose, and squinted. It was difficult to tell, but the pictures appeared to be men's photos. Was she on a dating app? Her body shook with another laugh, this one much louder.

The sound jerked him back to reality. He was staring too damn much and his syllabus would not finish itself. Samuel put his eyes back on his work and committed to fifteen more minutes of work before he rewarded himself with television. Except his TB Buddy made no effort to conceal her laughter. Whatever tickled her wasn't about to let up anytime too soon. The next time he glanced back at her, she had rolled over on her back and was giggling at her phone. The blue light shone against her brown skin, illuminating her wide grin. "Jesus Christ, Richard," she sighed before collapsing in another peel of laughter.

Who was Richard?

Samuel could have taken care of this distraction easily. A pair of earbuds were somewhere in his computer bag. Instead, he cleared his throat loudly. Yolanda made no sign that she had heard him. He tapped his fingers on his laptop, accepting that he wouldn't finish his syllabus tonight. He closed his computer and slipped it back into his bag.

"Are you going to bed?" she asked.

Samuel took off his glasses and rubbed his eyes. "Might as well," he said. "I can't concentrate."

"That happens to me all the time," she admitted, sitting up in bed. "I start stuff all the time and then get distracted. The last time that happened to me was when I made a pizza. I put the pie in the oven and was about to set a timer, but I texted Julia instead. After that, I think I started vacuuming my apartment because I stepped on a potato chip near the couch. I completely forgot about the pizza until I smelled it burning." She finished her story with a beaming smile.

Samuel couldn't help but ask, "So you ruined the pizza?"

Yolanda laughed. "That's not even the worst part. I couldn't reach my smoke detector, so I knocked it off the ceiling with my broom handle. Oh, you know what?" She returned to her phone. "Lemme make a note to get another smoke detector because it broke when it hit the floor."

He didn't realize he was frowning until she stopped talking. As he scrubbed a hand down his face, he pieced her story together. Potato chips on the floor, text messages with Julia, a broken smoke alarm, and a burned pizza. "Sounds very chaotic."

"That's very diplomatic of you," she teased. "I can see it on your face, Sam. You think my life is a mess."

If their shared bathroom was any indication, then yes, that's exactly what Samuel thought. But he went with diplomacy instead. "I've heard that chaos in the mind breeds creativity." He'd also heard that chaos bred poor impulse control, constant lateness, and sloppiness. But Samuel could almost excuse those problems when Yolanda smiled at him. It also helped that she was brilliant at her job and an impressive educator.

"All of that was to say: I understand distractions," she said.

"I'm usually good at staying focused..." He didn't want to come right out and say that *she* was the problem. "I usually work alone in my office."

She nodded solemnly. "So I should be more quiet?"

Samuel pressed his lips together and considered how to answer. "It's fine."

Yolanda raised a brow. "If you say so, Sam." She pushed herself out of bed and padded to the bathroom. "I'll turn in after this episode. Maybe getting to bed earlier isn't a bad idea."

Now Samuel felt guilty.

When she returned to her bed, Yolanda propped her laptop on her belly and continued watching her show.

"What are you watching?" he asked.

"*The Real Housewives of Atlanta*," she answered and immediately unplugged her headphone jack so he could hear the screaming argument.

"What are they fighting about?" Samuel asked as he laid on his side and watched the screen.

Yolanda turned the laptop around. "This one," she pointed at a white woman, "thinks she can sing but she absolutely can't. And this one used to be her friend and now they're not friends because she can't sing on her former friend's track."

"Huh." Samuel eased further into his blankets and rested his hand in the crook of his arm. "Why can't she be on the song?"

Yolanda set her phone on the nightstand. "Because she kept clowning Kim about how terrible her singing was. This isn't the first time she's been shady about the song. Anyway, Kim got fed up with the jabs and said, 'you can't be on the song.'"

As she explained the rest of the women on the show, Sam's brain shut off and his body relaxed. He got immersed into the barely-there plot and only interrupted to ask an occasional question. "Who's she, and why does she look so sad?"

"That's Cynthia, and she doesn't want to get married, but she will because what else is she going to do?"

"Mmh," he grunted. "She's very pretty."

"Gorgeous," Yolanda sighed. "She's a model."

Samuel didn't know how far into the episode he'd fallen asleep, but when he next awoke, the lights were off and Yolanda's back was to him as she lay sleeping. Her snoring, and the need to pee, jerked him awake. One of those issues, he could quickly take care of in the bathroom. The other... he'd have to find his earbuds and turn on his white noise app to drown out Yolanda.

But as far as first days go, it wasn't too bad.

Perhaps this week would turn out fine after all.

Chapter Three (Day 2: Human Knot)

The morning light was definitely an unwelcome intrusion.

If Yolanda had to guess, it was far earlier than ten am. Samuel, yanking back the curtains in what she also guessed was his passive aggressive attitude, didn't help either. She lifted her head and watched him walk away from the window after exposing their tiny cabin to daylight.

"What time is it?" she asked in a groggy voice.

"Eight-thirty," Samuel replied. He had already dressed himself in a pair of khaki shorts that came to the tops of his knees and a white polo shirt. Who wears white in the wilderness? A man who obsessed with maintaining order. There was no way a dude like Samuel would get a grass stain on his perfect white shirt.

Yolanda sat up in bed and checked her phone. Weren't they supposed to meet at the main lodge at nine am? "Why didn't you wake me up?" she asked, scrambling out of bed.

His dark brow arched as he ran a comb through his short hair, still wet from a shower. "I assumed that you had set an alarm like I did," he said in a neutral voice.

"I don't know why you'd assume that," Yolanda snapped as she moved around him to get to her dresser. Today's outfit, like all the others, would have to throw together quickly. There was barely enough time for her to take a shower. "You know I'm late to every committee meeting you chair, right?"

"True," he muttered. "I don't know what I expected."

His sarcasm made her grit her teeth as she stepped around him again. This goddamn room was too small for their simmering disdain. She couldn't stalk away with any flair. "Did you leave me any hot water?" she asked, on the way to the bathroom.

"I'm sure there's plenty," he said, checking his watch.

Yolanda rolled her eyes as she dumped her clothes on the toilet lid and searched for her shower soap. When she couldn't find it, her irritation spiked again. Samuel had moved everything around since she had last visited the bathroom. He had stacked her beauty products against the left side of the counter, against the wall. He based his stacking project on size, placing the smallest jars on the top of each tower. He lined the larger bottles up like little soldiers, closer to the mirrors, insuring all product labels facing outward. Like that psycho from *Sleeping with the Enemy*... "Sam?" she called out.

"Yes."

"What's your sign?"

There was a beat of silence before he came to the door. "Excuse me?"

With her hands planted on the bathroom counter, she looked at him through the mirror. "What's your sign?"

His eyes narrowed in confusion. "My zodiac sign?"

"Yes," she said, pointing to her carefully organized cosmetics. He glanced at them and frowned. "I'm a Virgo."

Oh boy, that explained everything. "I don't need you to do things like this," she said. "And now I can't find my shower

26

wash."

Samuel shrugged. "It's in the shower with my products," he said. "I was attempting to create order by placing things where they belonged. You'll find your loofah, shampoo, and conditioner in the shower as well." His tone suggested that his new system was obvious enough for a child to understand.

"I have my own order, thank you."

He approached the doorway and rested his forearm against the jamb. "Does it have anything to do with when you were born?" he asked with a smirk.

Yolanda stared at his full lips tug at the corner and ran her tongue across her teeth. *Don't you let him get under your skin, girl. You've got six more days with him.* "I'm sure it does," she said cooly, before closing the door on him.

After a hot shower, she hoped she would have a better outlook for the day. She quickly undressed and covered her hair with a shower cap that hung neatly in a curtain ring. *Oh, he's truly thought of everything...* Yolanda stuck her hand in to run the water and waited for a little steam. After a moment, she pulled the curtain aside and was about to take a step inside the tub. But before she could plant a foot, a black spot in the corner of her eye skittered along the white tiles.

Her entire body clenched in terror when she followed the movement. A silver-dollar-sized spider was running towards her direction. "Motherfucking sonofabitch!" she screamed as she jumped back. When her ass hit the counter behind her, she screamed again. "Oh my god, don't get me!"

Yolanda had enough sense to grab the nearest towel and clutch it to her front as she fumbled for the exit. She glanced over her shoulder to see if the arachnid was stalking her, but the shower curtain obscured his whereabouts. Knowing that she didn't have eyes on the suspect sent her into another screaming panic before pushing herself out the door and into the arms of her TB Buddy. "There's a fucking monster in there!" she cried as she scrambled around his body. That she was naked under her towel barely registered as Yolanda clutched the back of Samuel's shirt and hid from the Shower Creature.

"What is it?" he said, trying to keep the alarm from his own voice. He instinctively grabbed behind him as she shoved him forward.

When his warm hand connected with her bare thigh, she jumped again. "Sam!"

His hands went straight into the air when he realized his accidental grope. "Oh god, sorry," he apologized.

She quickly re-wrapped her towel and continued shaking like a leaf. "It's in there."

He was hesitant to enter the bathroom, even though she was practically shoving him in that direction. "What exactly is 'it' that's in the bathroom?"

"A spider tried to attack me," she whispered, as if the awful thing could hear her conspiring in the next room.

Samuel stopped his journey to the bathroom and lowered his hands. When he glanced over his shoulder, his confused eyes landed on her and narrowed. "A spider?"

"It's huge," she breathed. "And it was coming right at me like it had malice in its eyes."

This earned her a genuine belly laugh, the first she'd ever heard from Samuel Morris, and it was at her expense. "Malice? In all eight eyes?"

"Sam, it was running full-speed at me!" she hissed. Did he think she enjoyed being in the position of needing his help? "I need you to go in there—as my TB Buddy—to find it and kill it."

He stopped laughing long enough to approach the bathroom. "I value my neck for a lot more than three thousand bucks, chief," he said in a low growl. "I'll find him for three, but I'll catch and kill him, for ten."

Yolanda stopped dead in her tracks. "Are you quoting *Jaws* at me right now?"

Samuel glanced over his shoulder again. There was a twinkle in his eyes she'd never seen before. If she weren't so fucking frightened, she would have been attracted by how they lit up with humor. "According to you, this isn't like chasing bluegills and tommycocks. There's a man-killer in there."

Samuel Morris was never humorous. He'd never cracked a joke in all the time she'd known him. "Please, just get it."

"Yes, ma'am." He pulled himself out of her grasp and walked into the bathroom to inspect the scene. "There he is," he murmured as he squatted at the side of the tub.

"You see him?" she said, peaking around the door. "Are you fast enough to kill it?"

"I'm not going to kill it," he said. "I'll just move him outside."

"You're not fast enough!" she shouted.

"I am," he said, rising from the floor. When he reached for a fist-full of toilet paper, she let out a frustrated growl. There was no telling how late they would be for breakfast. "I'm just gonna catch him loosely."

She knew he'd never been fast enough for an assassin spider who wanted her blood. He got back down on his haunches and slowly approached the arachnid. The door obscured half of his body, and she refused to walk any closer.

She heard him grunt. "I missed," he called out.

Yolanda squealed as she leaped onto his bed. "I knew it!"

"Calm down in there," he said.

"Don't tell me to be calm!"

"I'm gonna try again."

Yolanda's heart thudded against her ribs as she listened out. Part of her knew that he would fail, the spider would run away, and would probably lay eggs in her ear tonight. The other part of him wished him luck, because he was the only person who could save her.

"Got him!" Soon, he was on the other side of the bathroom door, rushing out of the cabin with a wad of toilet paper. When Samuel returned, he closed the door behind him and tossed the paper in a nearby waste bin. When he looked up at her, he frowned. "What are you doing up there?"

She suddenly felt foolish, standing in the center of his bed with nothing but a towel covering her body. "You really got him?"

Samuel's eyes roamed over her body as he stuffed his hands in his pockets. "He put up a fight, but I got him. You're safe to shower, Yolanda."

Was Samuel Morris checking her out?

As his eyes met hers, he blushed and gave a forced cough. "Need help getting down?"

She shook her head while carefully climbing from his bed. "No, I'm good. Thank you." Yolanda couldn't help feeling a flicker of something between them as she retreated to the bathroom. He stepped back, giving her space to move around him, but a current of electricity passed from him, hitting her in the chest. The memory of his hand grazing her bare thigh came back to her as she peeked inside the bathroom. It wasn't an unpleasant sensation at all. Were it not for the awful circumstances, she might admit that she kind of liked his large

30

hand pressed against her skin.

"You're safe," he said as she peeked around the door. He returned to the brisk, business-like tone she was used to. It was almost disappointing to hear.

"Thank you," Yolanda said, breathing hard. A spider in the shower was not the wake up she wanted, but she was glad that he was there to assist her. Had it happened while she was alone, she would have definitely gone to Julia's cabin for all her hygiene needs.

"Yolanda?"

She paused at the doorway. "Yeah?"

The smallest smile creased the left side of his face. "What's *your* sign?"

Her skin flushed. "Leo," she croaked.

Samuel gave a thoughtful nod before turning his back to her. She watched in fascination as he began remaking his bed. Had she messed it up so badly? "Interesting…" he murmured. "Would not have guessed that."

* * *

"Who's ready for TB?" asked Craig and Joanne in unison.

Samuel cringed at their enthusiasm and phrasing. He couldn't blame Yolanda's snorted laugh. But he was already on edge since the spider incident caused them to be late for breakfast. Seeing his TB Buddy fly out of the bathroom wearing only a towel, did something unexpected to him. She moved too fast for him to divert his gaze, so he definitely caught a glimpse of her ass as she darted around him. When he touched her bare leg, a quick zing of arousal hit his belly and sent a shiver down

31

his back. To Samuel's disappointment, her skin was just as soft as he'd imagined...

Now the participants would partner with their TB Buddies for "an indoor, low-stakes TB Activity" that would help buddies get to know one another. Calling the activity "low-stakes" implied that higher-stakes were on the horizon, which made him nervous. How should he perform? He wasn't neurotic enough to believe Craig and Joanne had gold stars to pass out, but he *was* conditioned to strive towards perfection. He looked at his TB Buddy and wondered how that would actually pan out. Yolanda, who had quickly dressed in a pair of denim cut-offs and a black and yellow t-shirt that read "GIVE BEES A CHANCE," looked comfortable enough.

After breakfast, their boss shuttled everyone to another part of the main lodge, a yoga studio with mirrors affixed to the walls. While Dean Craig and Joanne spoke about the exciting week ahead of them, Yolanda busied herself in front of a mirror, adjusting the curls piled atop her head and checking her lipstick. If she worried about her appearance, Samuel thought she looked fine. Well, not just fine... Yolanda was beautiful. Even though it made them late, he especially liked those little swoopy things she did with her eye makeup. It made her look cat-like and mysterious.

"Get with your TB Buddy and take a seat on the floor," Joanne said. "If you're able to, I'd like you to face your buddy, legs criss-cross applesauce. When we're all situated, give me a hearty 'TB!'"

While he wanted to be a willing participant, Samuel refused to shout TB.

But Yolanda was already on the floor, crossing her legs and looking at him expectantly. When he followed her to the floor, she shouted, "We've got TB!"

"That's the spirit, Fox Cabin!" Joanne called out as someone near the back of the room, possibly Julia, cackled.

Yolanda raised a brow and threw him a smirk.

Okay, so his Buddy was a little competitive…

"Before we get started with our game, 'Winner/Loser,' we're just gonna take one minute to maintain steady eye contact with our buddies," Craig announced. "It's going to be awkward, but it's going to help you get comfortable with a person you probably don't know that well, yeah?"

Yolanda's smirk faded. "What?"

"Everyone get comfortable," Craig said. "I'm starting the timer… now!"

Samuel glanced around the room to see if everyone else was falling for this shit. The other TB Buddies went silent and faced each other, leaving him to face his own Buddy. Could he really spend the longest minute of his life staring into her eyes? When he met her gaze, he saw that she was just as uncomfortable. "We don't have to—"

She shook her head. "No, I plan on winning every single TB Activity this week. Stare into my eyes, Sam."

Samuel relaxed his shoulders and shook out his arms as he settled into the staring contest. As he tried steadying his breath, he took time to appreciate how dark Yolanda's eyes were. The brown hue bordered on black and was almost hypnotic. Her eyes were a comforting darkness that he could get lost in.

Whoa, that's weird.

Instead of getting lost, he focused his attention on the details around the windows to her soul. The tiny wrinkles at the corners of her eyes smoothed over when she wasn't grimacing at him. She had a tiny mole on the outside of her left eye, just

33

below the cat-eye swoop. It made her look very sophisticated. He let his eyes drop to her cute, pert nose before settling on her mouth. She wore a deep wine lipstick that complemented her smooth nut-brown skin perfectly.

"Eyes back up here," she whispered.

Samuel returned to her eyes. "Sorry, I got distracted."

"Mmh."

He sighed, returning to her intense gaze.

"All right, guys," Craig said. "Minute's up! How did that feel?"

The room filled with murmurs of affirmation. Yolanda rolled her eyes. "I'm ready for the next activity," she muttered.

"Okay, we're going to play Winner/Loser with our partners," Joanne said. "In this game, one person will tell their Buddy about a negative memory, nothing too personal. Their partner will take their story and put a positive spin on it! See? Winners/Losers. Take turns with that."

Samuel searched his mind for something that wasn't too negative or too personal. But Yolanda beat him to the punch. "I'll go first," she said.

"Okay…"

"Once there was this grant that I applied for," she started, "I thought if I got it, the English Department majors would get free laptops. Some of my first-generation students are also from low-income families, and the added technology would have helped them with their studies," Yolanda finished her story with pursed lips. "I didn't get the grant."

Samuel narrowed his eyes. Of course she didn't get the grant… because he had. He'd applied to the Wilson-Kramer Grant a year ago with the same aim. He, too, had low-income history majors who struggled to keep up with their studies. He didn't know who else he had competed with because when

Samuel won something, he hurried on to the next thing. The way she recited this memory told him two things: first, she knew that he got the grant; and second, she was still sore about it. Was this why she disliked him?

"Okay… a positive spin," he murmured. "Well, like anything you lose out on, that disappointment offers a valuable lesson on how to approach the next prize, yeah? Next time, you'll know how to follow directions better or learn what works best for professional writing situations," he paused to think. "Are you sure you sent it off on time?"

Yolanda tilted her head to the side as she regarded him. "You're actually serious."

He nodded. "I am." His advice sounded positive to him…

"Wow," she sighed, rolling her eyes. "I teach professional writing."

"Huh, I thought you were a literature professor."

She threw her hands up. "I teach both, Sam. Tell me your negative memory."

Yolanda confused him. "My positive spin wasn't helpful enough?"

"It sounded condescending as hell," she whispered. "Sent it off on time? Follow directions? You make me sound like one of my students."

His face reddened. "I didn't mean to make it sound like that, Yolanda. That's just what I would do if I were in your shoes. I'd spend the week reviewing what I did wrong, and then I'd probably attend a grant-writing workshop."

She stilled. "We have those?"

"Ted Hanover, at the Writing Center, has those seminars and workshops for faculty development. He sends out an email once a month."

Yolanda's arms loosened their tight grip across her chest as she blushed. "Oh."

"Next time I see him, I'll tell him to add you to the email list."

Her face dipped as she scratched the back of her neck. "I'm already on it," she muttered in a quiet voice.

"Huh?" Samuel leaned closer to hear her.

"I'm on his list," she said in a clearer voice. "I started sending the emails to a spam folder a few months ago."

He sat back and nodded. "Gotcha."

"You go to those things?" she asked with a raised brow.

"I go to Ted because writing doesn't come naturally to me," Samuel admitted. "I have to practice and I take the help when I can get it."

Yolanda's face softened. "Oh. I see."

He was also starting to see. Yolanda Watson held grudges like no one else he knew. That she'd let something this small root her in the past was a bit strange. "I guess I'll describe my negative memory."

"Go ahead."

"I had a hard time keeping control of my Assessment Committee last semester. I had to table many of my goals because of interruptions. No one seemed like they wanted to be there, and the professors who *did* attend the meetings were constantly late." When he finished, he took a deep breath.

Yolanda's eyebrows knitted in the middle as she stared at him. When realization eventually dawned on her face, she chuckled behind her hand. "Oh my god, Sam. Are you really in your feelings about assessment criteria?" she asked. "Of course no one wanted to go to those meetings."

"They're mandatory," he said in a low voice. "The committees are a part of our service to the university."

"Shit, I know that; everyone knows that," she said. "But between classes, departmental meetings, and office hours, those meetings are really low on my list of priorities."

Samuel blew a frustrated sigh at the ceiling. "Is that your positive spin?"

She shrugged. "We got through it and now it's over?"

"You were one of those late people!"

"Hey, Fox Cabin?" Joanne called out. "That doesn't sound like TB spirit to me…"

"I'm sorry, Joanne," Yolanda replied. "My TB Buddy and I are trying our best to be positive about TB."

"Stop calling it that," Samuel snapped.

"That's what it's called!"

Dean Craig climbed from the floor and clapped his hands. "Maybe that means we're ready for our next TB Activity."

Samuel was ready to throw in the towel. They weren't ready to stare into each other's eyes, nor were they ready to listen to one another. He was clearly dealing with a child who couldn't take anything seriously.

Chapter Four

I n an open field, sandwiched between the cabins and the tree line of Redstone's forest, Franklin University employees waited for further TB Activity instruction. After their little outburst in the yoga room, Yolanda and Samuel made all efforts to keep their distance. He stood off by himself while Yolanda sat in the grass.

Instead of helping one another, their talks devolved into bickering. She had almost expected it, but it still surprised her how upset Samuel was about their shared committee experience. She didn't think Assessment Criteria was that important... Unless it was the order and control Samuel needed. Judging by how he had organized her toiletries, it made sense.

"This seat taken?"

Yolanda looked up to see Julia blocking out most of the sun with a wide-brimmed straw hat. "Help yourself."

Her friend sat beside her and ran her fingers through the thick grass. "So what was that back there?"

She shrugged. "He's in his feelings about a committee we were on."

"I think that was the point of the exercise," Julia said dryly. "Did you listen to what he said and put a positive spin on it?"

Yolanda thought about it. "I guess not."

"Hmm."

"How did staring into Brenda's eyes go?" Yolanda asked.

Julia chuckled. "Awkward at first, but I eventually settled into it. I learned that she had a rough summer with her parakeet dying."

"Aww, that's hella sad," Yolanda said with a frown. "What was your positive spin?"

Her friend smiled serenely. "I told her that birds are really smart, and Lucas was probably smart enough to know his human was a kind woman. I'll bet he had a lovely life with her."

Yolanda stared at Julia. "That sounds really nice, Jules."

She shrugged. "Losing a pet is hard. Brenda from Communications isn't bad."

"No, she's not."

"How was it staring into Sam's eyes?"

"Easy," Yolanda answered quickly. "He's got pretty eyes."

"Excuse me?"

"I can be objective."

Julia's smug expression was one of her more insufferable looks. To avoid it, Yolanda sought Samuel's location. He was still on the periphery of the large group, staring at the ground. As he bent at the waist to pick up a rock, his white polo rode up his torso exposing defined oblique muscles. He examined the rock in his hands for a few moments before throwing it towards the edge of the forest. She watched as he wiped his hands on khaki pants and sighed.

She didn't blink until Julia's fingers snapped in her face. "Girl, I was talking to you."

Yolanda jumped. "I'm listening."

"Mhh-hmm."

Thankfully, Joanne interrupted their conversation with a well-timed Hearty TB. "All right, gang, let's hustle up for the next activity!"

Yolanda pushed herself off the ground and pulled Julia up with her. "Do you think there's something going on between Joanne and Craig?"

Her friend nodded. "I absolutely think there's something going on between our dean and his secretary," she whispered. "No middle-aged adults could ever get excited about TB without fucking."

"I think it's kind of cute," Yolanda said. "He's a widower right?"

"And according to Brenda, Joanne's divorce was finalized over the summer."

Yolanda raised a brow. "Okay now, come through divorce. Maybe they should be the ones sharing a cabin."

They shared a chuckle as they entered the large group. Samuel glanced over at them, but his expression was placid and brief. He dug his hands in his pockets and faced the front. She couldn't articulate why, but that action annoyed the hell out of Yolanda. She always caught him staring at her, usually while she was having a laugh. Was he really so opposed to humor?

Craig stood beside Joanne, ready to jump in. "Okay guys, the next TB Activity is called The Human Knot. In our group of eighteen, we need to split off into three groups of six. Can everybody do that now?"

Yolanda took Julia's hand and dragged her to the nearest clump of people. "We're a group," she called out.

"That's the TB spirit, Fox Cabin," Julia mocked.

Their small group comprised of Brenda from Communications, Sarah from English, and Dennis from Philosophy. They still needed a sixth person. Before Yolanda could point that out, Dennis called over to Samuel, who surveyed the forming groups. "Get over here, Morris."

Samuel took his sweet time getting to the group, but once he did... he gave Yolanda another intense look. This time she didn't feel quite as annoyed. She could have been imagining it, but his expression was almost smoldering. Or was he just angry with her? "Thanks," he muttered.

"We've got groups of six?" Craig asked. "Fantastic. Now what we're going to do is stand in a circle." They formed circles. "Look at the person standing opposite of you." Yolanda looked at Samuel, who stood on the opposite side of the circle, and took a deep breath. "Take that person's hand with *your* left hand." She took his hand; it was sweaty. "Now go ahead and use your right hand to take someone else's hand." Yolanda's right hand connected with Sarah's. "Now... while your hands are together, you must work together to untangle yourselves. If anyone releases a grip, your team must start over. But..." Craig made sure he had everyone's attention. "The first team who untangles themselves is getting..."

Yolanda craned over her shoulder to look at her boss. "Getting what?"

"A bottle of champagne!" Joanne cried.

"Wait, we're getting prizes for these activities?" Peter from Theology called out.

Craig looked mighty proud of himself. "Joanne and I came up with some nice prizes for the week."

Well, that changes the stakes....

"You guys ready?" Joanne asked. "Can I get a 'TB'?"

"TB!" they cried unanimously.

"Okay guys," Dennis said. "Let's go slow."

41

"Your hat is a liability," Yolanda said as she tried dodging Julia's wide-brim.

"My hat is keeping me safe from the sun's UV-rays," Julia corrected.

"I really wouldn't mind that drink tonight," Brenda said.

Yolanda didn't so much care about the champagne as she did about dominating the competition. "I'm moving in this direction," she told her team. "Follow me, Sarah."

As she pulled her arm over Dennis' head, Sarah yelped. "Nope. That won't work."

"Hold on, Yolanda," Samuel said. "I'm going this way."

"You can't go that way," Yolanda said.

"Wait," Julia said, ducking her head. "If you two kneel for a second, I'm going to step over your arms."

Most of the group lowered themselves so Julia could test her theory. While connected to Brenda and Dennis, she loosened the knot slightly, giving them some breathing room. They needed to take a beat to examine where Julia had taken them, but before Yolanda could speak, Samuel twisted his body, bringing her closer to him.

"No, unwind, Sam."

"I think if I just…" He twisted her arm before pausing. "Okay never mind."

Brenda raised the arm connected to Dennis and safely crossed over Julia's enormous sun hat. "Julia, this hat is a bit much."

"This hat is fine!" Julia said, ducking.

"Okay, team," Dennis said, in his football coach's voice. "So now I need Morris to take Watson's arm and loop it over Crawford's giant hat."

"Where's Sarah gonna go?" Yolanda asked.

42

"We'll find out," Dennis replied.

She and Samuel raised their joined hands over Julia's head until Yolanda's arms crossed over her chest and she faced the outside of the circle. "Am I supposed to go this way?" she asked.

"Obviously not," Samuel said.

She shot him a glare.

"Alright, hold on," Sarah said with a giggle. "I'm also criss-cross applesauce."

Her phrasing caused the group to erupt in giggles. Except for Samuel. "Let's focus up," he said in his teacher's voice.

Yolanda groaned. "We're trying to have a little fun, Sam."

"I understand that," he said in a measured voice. "But we have an objective."

Her head dropped backwards as she rolled her eyes. "Whatever."

"Sam, duck under my arm," Julia instructed. "I'm tryna see something."

Samuel followed her directions, but twisted Yolanda's arm. "No, that won't work. Sarah needs to unwind herself so we can see where Yolanda goes."

Sarah untied herself and faced the inside of the circle, but she spun Yolanda into Samuel's solid chest. The sturdy wall of muscle almost knocked the breath out of her upon impact. A shiver went down her back as she met his warm torso. Instinctively, she looked over her shoulder at his face. His eyes met hers and his strong jaw clenched. Just seeing the small movement in his face sent a wave of arousal through her body. *WTF?*

Dennis spoke up next. "Gibson is straight, but we've got a situation with Watson and Morris."

You damn right there was a situation. Something about being

43

pressed against his front was doing something to her body that she didn't appreciate. She had been close to him in their cabin, when she was ordering him to kill a spider, but this position was quite different. She wasn't in control.

A powerful gust of wind blew through the field, lifting Julia's hat away from her head. Instead of letting it fly away, Julia yelped and released Dennis' hand. Before anyone could stop her from upsetting the group's delicate balance, Julia pitched forward and toppled them like dominoes. Dennis went down first, and Brenda followed.

Samuel fell backwards with Yolanda in his grip. She twisted just in time to land face-first on top of him. Together, they hit the grass with a hard "oomph." Sarah was the only one who stayed on her feet as Julia crawled off Dennis. "I got that hat at Neiman Marcus," she cried in the distance.

"We win!" Peter Leonard called out. "We win!"

Yolanda barely heard the other team's cheers because she was in a solid trap between Samuel's powerful arms and chest. He'd caught her as she fell upon him. They laid in the grass, face to face, breathing hard. "Are you okay?" she whispered.

His eyes darted between her eyes and her mouth. "Yes," he said in a husky voice. "Are you?"

Let's see… She planted her hands on his pecs, trying not to massage the firm muscles beneath her sweaty palms. Yolanda tried not to do a lot of things in that moment: *Don't touch his face, don't look at his lips, and do NOT move your hips.* "I'm fine," she breathed.

His hands were at her ribs, but they moved downward. His heavy palms traced a slow path along her sides until they reached her hips. Yolanda sucked in a breath as she quietly followed the sensation in her mind. "I'm just gonna…" he trailed off, as he lifted her pelvis away from his.

When she realized what he was doing, her face burned with embarrassment. "Oh my god," she said. "I'm sorry if I hurt—"

"—No," he said, squeezing his eyes shut. "It's fine—"

She scrambled away from him, finding safety in the grass. "Did I—"

"—Yolanda, you're fine," he said, sitting up.

She snuck a covert glance to his pants and noticed his discreet adjustment to the crotch as he sat criss-cross applesauce. "I'm going to help Julia find that fucking hat."

He nodded with tightly pressed lips. "Sounds good."

Jesus Christ... Yolanda pulled herself from the ground and went after her friend, who was chasing down a hat in the Wisconsin fields. Their team lost champagne, Julia lost her hat, and Yolanda gained a bunch of questionable feelings. Most of them made her hot in the face, her breasts heavy, and arousal uncoil within her womb.

Hearty TB, my ass.

* * *

"What did I learn today?" Samuel muttered to himself as he jotted notes on Joanne's Daily Reflection questionnaire.

- *My partner is a Leo and deathly afraid of spiders... extremely competitive*
- *I didn't feel listened to during Winner/Loser*
- *The Human Knot game was disastrous*
- *I'm not sure what I'm supposed to get out of this week.*

Samuel folded his paper in half and waited for Joanne to come by and collect it. He was ready to retreat into the Fox Cabin and sleep off Day Two of the retreat. This was more human interaction that he was accustomed to, and the stimulation was already exhausting him.

"What did you write?" Yolanda asked, peeking at his paper.

"That's between me and Joanne," he said, folding it over once again.

She rolled her eyes and returned to her own paper. As she wrote, Samuel noted how tightly she gripped the ink pen in her left hand. He didn't know why her being a lefty interested him. He'd always heard that left-handed people were more creative and artsy, but thought the "science" was bunk. He watched her hand drag across wet ink, smudging her words as she went. He wondered if he should write that observation down as well.

No, let it go.

There were other, more disturbing, things he'd learned while they spent the day together. When Yolanda fell on top of him, he learned that his first instinct was to hold her tight, protecting her from the dirt. There was a grass stain on his white polo that he'd have to blot with his stain-removing pen. He also learned that their bodies fit and locked together perfectly in his snug grip. They fit so well that it scared the shit out of him. Why hadn't he let Yolanda believe that she'd accidentally kneed him in the balls instead of acting like a weirdo? The way she had scrambled away from him made him feel like a lech.

If he embarrassed her, she didn't let on while they wrote their reflections in the main lodge's cafeteria. She was back to her eye-rolling ways. Finally, she set her pen down, her pinkie knuckle smudged black, and folded her paper. "Done," she announced. "Ready to get home, TB Buddy?"

Samuel gave her a surprised nod. He never knew how she felt, but right now, she didn't seem worried about today's events.

"Sure."

Joanne collected their papers, and they excused themselves back to their cabins. In the darkness, they quietly walked down the path to their cabin. Redstone Retreat was quite a lovely spot in the Wisconsin woods. Samuel could feel himself getting acclimated to an environment outside the bustling city. Chicago was a great place to live, but escaping to the quiet was also nice. The warm glow of lanterns and the occasional lightning bug lit their way back "home," as Yolanda called it. He had to hold back his laughter as firefly flitted past her face, making her yelp and bump into him. He took her by the shoulders and put her back on her side of the path. "You're okay," he murmured.

"Sorry, I just don't like bugs," she said.

"You're going to have a rough time this week."

"I'm also sorry about today."

"What did you do?" he asked as they approached Fox Cabin.

She shrugged. "I don't think I was very understanding when you described your negative memory. I shouldn't have laughed and I shouldn't have brushed you off like that."

He looked at her. "Thank you for saying that."

Yolanda unlocked their cabin and turned the light on. She did a quick survey of the bathroom, just to make sure the coast was clear. When she returned to the main room. "You think the spider came back?"

In the spirit of not laughing at one another, Samuel simply shook his head as he closed the door. "I don't think so. But if it does, I'll move it back outside."

"It's easier if you kill them," she said, kicking her shoes off. They landed near her bed in two different spots, but Samuel tried to let it go.

He sat on his bed and removed his shoes before tucking them in front of his nightstand. "Killing spiders is bad luck."

Yolanda shook with revulsion. "Okay, we can disagree about that but I'll be grateful if you remove them all the same." She dropped onto her bed and hugged her legs to her chest. As they faced each other in the dim light of the cabin, she flashed him a bright smile. "You mind if I try again?"

"Try what?"

"Giving you a positive spin."

Samuel could have sworn he felt something in his chest. Had his heart literally leaped at her words? He almost told her to forget about it, but stopped himself. Yolanda was *trying*. "Sure, I guess so," he said nonchalantly.

"All right. I think I should have said thank you for taking the committee work seriously. Without your labor, we probably wouldn't have finished many of the tasks. You have a knack for administrative work that I don't have. And instead of learning from you, I flaked."

He coughed and rubbed his palms on his thighs. "Uh... thank you for being honest with me." He *was* thankful to hear her admit to her insecurities. And it prompted him to admit something in return. "Maybe I should learn how to relax a little."

She grinned. "Just a little."

A muffled chirp went off somewhere from her bed, interrupting their moment. Samuel exhaled as she rolled over and retrieved her phone. "Oh fuck, it's Richard again."

Samuel's heart fell at the mention of another man, which was puzzling because her personal life was none of his concern. "Who's Richard?" he still asked.

She gave an exasperated sigh while scrolling through her

phone. "He's the fool I'm trolling on Tinder."

"You troll people on Tinder?"

"Regularly," she said, moving from her bed to his. When Yolanda sat beside him, she was so close that their thighs touched. "Here's a virtual harem of dudes I've matched up with only to find out they ain't shit."

Samuel's heart lifted again and began galloping in his chest. Her thigh. His thigh. Were pressed together.

Warmth flowed from her body, directly to his, and set his face aflame. While she scrolled through her private messages, he leaned closer for a better look and ended up smelling her hair. Samuel let his eyes fall shut for a brief second and allowed himself to inhale a gentle fragrance of coconut. "A harem?"

"Well, there's only four of them now, Mike must have given up today. I gave him the Uncomfortable Questionnaire, and he dropped out after eight questions."

When he got a look at her messages with Mike, he laughed. "You asked him 'what age were you when you realized your parents were no longer your heroes?' My god, that's rough."

She flashed him an impish smile. "Too much?"

"Just a little. What did you do to Richard?"

Yolanda switched to another screen. "I've been feeding him lines from the movie *Apocalypse Now*. Actually, you could help me with that, Mr. Vietnam War Scholar," she said, nudging his shoulder.

He returned her smile. "I don't know…"

"Come on," she nudged again. "I've already exhausted *Full Metal Jacket*."

Against his better judgement, Samuel took her phone and scrolled through her conversation with Richard. "He's asked you for a nude," he said, cringing.

"That's not the first time."

"What did you send him?" he asked, both curious and nervous by how she'd answer.

"A photo of a cat with a ball of yarn," she chuckled. "He said he wanted to see pussy-play."

Samuel choked. "Jesus, what?"

"Have you never been on a dating app? This is how men behave."

He knew he would never be that bold. As shy and anxious as he was, he couldn't imagine demanding something that… private from a woman. "And he's still talking to you?"

"Go figure," she shrugged.

Samuel was amazed by how this day was ending. She had apologized for minimizing his feelings, and now they were sharing an intimate laugh on *his* bed. "Fine, I'll help." He closed out of her app and Googled a picture of Willem Dafoe, kneeling in the mud with his arms raised above him. "You mind?"

She giggled and leaned closer, her breasts pressing against his bicep. "Oh my god, why?"

"Just to see what he says."

"Go ahead."

He saved it to her photos and went back to Tinder. The screen revealed her profile page. There was a lovely picture of her sitting atop a bicycle in a flowery sundress and white sneakers. She'd pinned her curly hair into a high bun and decorated it with small white flowers. Her profile read: *Yolanda Watson 38, Chicago, Looking for a man who enjoys talking about movies, books, and politics without inserting "well actually" into the conversation. I love to cook, play with puppies, and yoga. Make me laugh and I'll make you curry.* "I didn't realize we were the same age," he said.

"How old did you think I was?" she asked.

"I'm not sure. Just younger, I guess." He went back to the private messages with Richard and uploaded Willem Dafoe's photo into the chat. "And now we wait."

"So you've never used one of these apps?" she asked.

Samuel shook his head, afraid to admit that he hadn't been on a date in a couple years.

"How do you meet people?" she pressed.

He quietly regarded her before answering. She seemed genuinely curious about the state of his love-life. "I've been throwing myself into my work."

Her dark brown eyes fell to his mouth. "Sounds kinda lonely."

It was.

He shrugged. "I manage."

"No man's an island, Sam," she said, nudging his shoulder.

"There's got to be a better way than this," he gestured to the phone. "Do you actually get any keepers from Tinder?"

"I get by, I suppose," she admitted with a shrug. "It's just a tool for hooking up. If I have an itch that needs scratching, I'll hit up one of these guys."

Samuel was now very curious about her itches... "Yeah?"

But before she could answer, her phone beeped loudly. "It's Richard."

Fucking Richard... He read the message and chuckled.

wut??

"You want me to reply?"

"Go ahead, I'm interested to see where this goes."

He typed, *Adagio for Strings is my favorite song; what's your favorite song?* "How's that?" he asked, showing her the message.

"Not bad," she said with an appreciative nod. "Not bad at all, Padawan."

"Surely he's done now?"

51

Yolanda scoffed. "As a man, you should know men better. He's not going to be done for a while."

Strangely, he found himself not done with her either. Samuel had began to see how she lured people to her. Yolanda was a messy storm who hated spiders and committee work, but she was charming as hell. She took the phone from him and closed out of the app.

"I'll let him think on that for a while," she said, standing from his bed. He felt her absence immediately. "What are you going to do for the rest of the night?"

His brain struggled to switch topics so quickly. One minute, they were sitting together; the next minute, he had to figure out how to preoccupy himself without her. He didn't like how startling it felt. "I was going to work on my syllabus," he lied.

"I'm going to watch more *Real Housewives*," she said, tossing her phone on her bed before wandering to the bathroom. "I'll try to set an alarm for the morning."

Samuel watched her disappear into the bathroom. "Sounds good," he said in a voice that sounded too eager, even for him.

Chapter Five (Day 3: Scavenger Hunt)

Y ou down with TBB?" Joanne chanted as she crossed her arms over her chest. She wore a pair of sunglasses and a backward ball cap, and no one could laugh. In a room full of cynical Gen-Xers, no one could laugh at the display at the front of Redstone's craft room.

"Yeah, you know me!" cried Craig. As his skinny arms "raised the roof," Yolanda willed herself not to look at Julia. If she had, she would have lost it. She bit her lips and tried not to cry as her boss and his secretary took them back to the '90s.

"Who's down with TBB?"

"The Hu-man-i-ties!"

Yolanda began clapping loudly to cover the sound of her choked laughter. "Yaasss! Get it!" Luckily, Samuel and the rest of her table joined in with the same idea of ending this magical music journey into the past.

"Okay, gang!" Joanne said, taking off her sunglasses and hooking them into the collar of her t-shirt. "Now that Craig and I have *pumped up the jams*, it's time to tell you all why you've got marshmallows and spaghetti on your tables."

She could have guessed why a bag of marshmallows and dry pasta were on their table. Her group of colleagues would have to build a tower in an allotted amount of time. Sarah had already ripped a hole in the bag and popped several marshmallows in her mouth when she thought no one was watching. Yolanda shot her a grin. "You're eating a TB Activity," she whispered.

The red-head crossed her blue eyes and stuck her tongue out. "You can't expect me to sit here and *not* eat free marshmallows."

Their group was the same as yesterday's, except Dennis from Philosophy had been switched out for Peter from Theology, much to Julia's chagrin. Without thinking, Yolanda had immediately found a seat next to Samuel upon entering the craft room. Perhaps she was used to getting close to him? They grew closer last night after she apologized for her behavior. They actually shared a laugh over her Tinder profile, something she hadn't expected.

Yolanda may have been flirting with him... just a bit. But she couldn't help nudge him when she heard his soft inhale as he looked over her shoulder. She teased him some more just to see his smile and blush. He was even more handsome when his jaw stopped clenching in irritation. She had hoped his relaxed demeanor would last while they were in front of others. His instinct to clam up around their colleagues was noticeable. Even now, as he watched Sarah sneak marshmallows like a cute mouse, his lips were pressed in a thin line.

"Whichever team builds the highest free-standing structure in eighteen minutes will win a special advantage for the next activity," Craig said. "On your tables, you have all the tools you'll need: One jumbo marshmallow, one bag of mini-puffs, and twenty sticks of spaghetti. However you choose to use them is up to your group, but *every* structure must have the large marshmallow on the very top. TB?"

Since "TB" was quickly becoming a part of their collective

vernacular, the unison reply was immediate. "TB!"

"On your marks, get set, go!" Joanne said, pressing the button on her stopwatch.

At their table, Sarah tore the bag of marshmallows open wider and spilled them onto the surface. "I only ate three," she said. "We oughta be fine."

"We should create a wide base for support," Samuel said in an authoritative voice.

"That will take too long," Yolanda said as she pictured a tower in her mind. "We need to go with a simple design. Everyone should just start building cubes and we'll stack them."

Samuel scoffed. "With the large marshmallow on top? It'll topple as soon as we try to connect it."

Brenda broke a stick of spaghetti in half. "How about we make a cubed base, but criss-cross the insides?"

"Why would you break that before we could come up with basic measurements?" Samuel asked with a frown.

Brenda blanched as she held a piece of spaghetti in either hand. "I just thought we should get started..."

Yolanda frowned at Samuel. "She's right, we have to start eventually."

The clench in his jaw returned.

"What if we make a pyramid for the base?" Peter suggested. "It worked for the Pharaoh."

"Jesus Christ, Peter," Julia said, rolling her eyes.

"Holy Moses, you mean," he corrected.

The joke helped lift the mood that Samuel was so hell-bent to dampen with his seriousness. Their little group was not only laughing at Peter but also at Julia's annoyed reaction.

"If we start with a pyramid where do we go from there?" Samuel asked, cutting the laughter short.

Brenda had quietly put her pieces of dry pasta on the table and placed her hands in her lap. Yolanda couldn't help but notice her silent defeat. She'd seen similar dynamics in her own classroom. In every group, there was always a student who ran roughshod over their peers. Sam's unwavering obsession with getting tasks completed would ultimately silence his teammates.

"I think Brenda has already gotten us started," Yolanda said, taking the broken pasta. "We can start with a four corner pyramid, this size, and see where we get from there."

"We'll waste resources if we don't know what comes after a pyramid," Samuel argued.

"We're wasting time if we keep sitting here talking about it," Sarah said, popping another mini-puff in her mouth. "That's four."

"Ease up on our building materials," Julia laughed.

"Okay, Brenda and Peter, you guys build a pyramid based on what's already measured out."

"I'm not seeing a lot being built over here," Joanne said in a sing-song voice. "You guys have twelve minutes…"

"This table is working hard," Craig called out. "They look like they're four inches high."

"I think we should start off with a pentagon," Samuel said. "If we have time to add a pyramid near the top, maybe that will work. But we absolutely need a decent foundation."

"Show of hands," Yolanda said. "Who thinks that we have enough resources for a five-sided shape as a base?"

No one raised their hands.

"I think a cube might be better," Julia said with a shrug. "I'm gonna build one real quick."

Samuel crossed his arms over today's polo shirt: green. "So

we're building separate structures?"

"Sam, this isn't a *Bridge on a River Kwai*," Yolanda sighed. "It's just spaghetti and marshmallows."

"Wait, I've got it," Sarah said, jumping up from her seat, popping yet another mini-puff in her mouth. "One giant pyramid. Let's make sure the base already has height to it."

"Okay, that could work," Peter said, taking four large sticks and connecting them with mini puffs. When their base was complete, Brenda added four more sticks for the walls and connected them with a single mini-puff.

"Seven minutes," Joanne called out.

They had a giant pyramid, but nothing else.

"What if…" Julia stood over the structure and tested the top of it. Once she judged it strong enough, she took a small piece of spaghetti and connected the top with another mini-puff.

"What are you thinking?" Yolanda asked.

"Give me some more sticks," her friend said.

Peter handed her a handful of noodles.

"I'm gonna jam two sticks in this little guy to start a tower," Julia said.

"I don't think that will hold," Samuel warned.

"But if you stick four noodles in one mini-puff, creating a tiny four-post support…" Peter trailed off as he jabbed sticks into his own marshmallow. "Yes, yes. This could work."

Samuel stood over Peter's work with a judgmental stare. "That's not enough support for the immense weight of—"

"Oh my god, Sam," Yolanda said with an exasperated sigh. "If you don't give people a chance to fuck up, they won't learn how to find different paths to success."

"Oh wow, that's a good observation on leadership," Craig said as he passed their dysfunctional table. "Way to TB, Fox Cabin.

Four minutes, gang!"

Samuel raised a dark brow at her as he pursed his lips. He crossed his arms over his chest and took a step away from Peter's work. "Fine," he said in a low voice.

Oh great, now he was going to pout. With four minutes left on the clock, she didn't have time to coddle Samuel's feelings in a group setting. "Okay, if Peter connects the four-posts to the large marshmallow, maybe we can put it on the great pyramid."

Samuel stayed quiet.

But Brenda shook her head. "Sam might be right. This adds weight to the pyramid. Can we try just one noodle with the large puff?"

"Try it," Julia said. "We've got how many minutes to make up our minds?"

"Two or three," Sarah said.

Samuel couldn't help himself. "Yes, but you're trying to trade weight for stability when the base won't allow for either."

Yolanda bit her tongue. As far as she was concerned, she was the leader of this little group and her duty was to ensure that everyone tried something that fit their creative needs. That meant letting Samuel say his piece while other people worked.

As the group raised Brenda's idea of a tower, Yolanda looked around the other tables to see her colleagues laughing and having a good time. Her group was just serious. Marshmallow-tower building was supposed to be fun and her group wasn't having it. Of course, Brenda's tower toppled over in the first attempt, and she was done participating.

"One minute…" Craig called out.

"Okay, let's do this," Julia said, sticking a small post in the top of their pyramid. "While I hold this little puff, I need Peter to jam this tower on top. Aim correct, Pete."

Peter positioned himself over the pyramid and took a deep breath. "Keep it steady," he said, making contact with the marshmallow.

"Shove it in there, Pete." Julia urged.

Any other time, Yolanda would have clowned her friend for her word choice. But right now? They were so intensely focused on making this work, their group stood around the table like scientists at Cape Canaveral. She didn't want to say anything to jinx the progress.

When Peter pushed four dry noodles into Julia's mini puff, they looked at each other and Yolanda swore she saw more than Marshmallow Tower hopes. Their eyes read something much more meaningful.

"Thirty seconds!"

"Let it go?" Julia asked in a hushed voice.

Peter gave her a quiet nod. After a few seconds, he pulled his hands away. They all watched as the tower... stood. Whatever collective breath they had held, everyone exhaled *away* from the structure.

"Holy shit," Sarah said.

"We did it," Brenda breathed.

Julia and Peter exchanged a weird smile, while Samuel shook his head. "That's not going to hold," he muttered under his breath.

"That's time," Joanne cried. "Step away from your towers."

"I'm coming around with my tape measure," Craig warned. "I hope everyone is ready..."

Yolanda wanted him to hurry it along because she believed that Samuel was right. Anything could topple their janky structure; a sneeze or a dirty look. But she didn't want Samuel to be right about this one thing. He brought his stringent logic to a space where the participants were supposed to have a little fun.

She watched Craig measure the first table. "Fourteen inches over here, and things look a little precarious..."

Their structure had to have been at least eighteen inches.

He carefully stretched his tape measure along the side of the second group's structure as everyone watched in intense silence. "Sixteen inches, mark that down, Joanne!"

As Craig left their table and walked to her group's she glanced at their tower and saw a dramatic lean. She crossed her arms and stared at the large puff on top, willing it to stay put, but it sank. Like the slowest car accident in the world, all the eyewitnesses stood by shouting for the inevitable not to happen.

"Craig hurry up!" Peter shouted.

"Here I come..."

But it was too late. Their tower dipped and fell away from the pyramid, landing in a soft thud against the table.

"Oh, guys," Craig murmured. "It looks like you didn't make it, huh?"

"I knew it wouldn't hold," Samuel sighed.

"Okay, fine," Yolanda snapped. "But are you being a buzz-kill on purpose?"

Samuel's expression was a mix of shock and hurt, both emotions she wasn't sure he was capable of. "I was trying to tell you and you didn't listen," he said.

"It's my job to listen to all of the voices at this table," she countered.

"Interesting," Craig nodded between the participants. "So who do you think was the leader of this table?"

"I was," she and Samuel said together.

The rest of the group looked at them in confusion.

"You thought you were the leader?" Samuel asked her with a raised brow.

"Of course," she replied. "How did you think *you* were the leader?"

"I was trying to lead until you began interrupting," he said with his hands on his hips. "Which is usually what happens when we work together."

The hush that fell over the table made Yolanda's face burn with embarrassment. Instead of engaging with his retort, she turned to Craig and smiled sweetly. "There you have it. We both contributed to the failure of our team."

Craig nodded. "And that's an awesome observation to make, Fox Cabin. Sometimes we get so caught up in our roles as leaders we forget to listen to those around us."

She ran her tongue over her teeth so she didn't groan out loud.

She thought they had developed a truce the night before. She and Samuel shared a laugh, alone in the dim light of their cabin. While isolated from the rest of the world, they could see eye-to-eye. But now? Their truce was as flimsy as spaghetti and marshmallow puffs.

"Everyone take a thirty-minute break, and then we'll meet outside the main lodge for our next TB Activity," Craig said, clapping at their progress. "We'll also announce the advantage our winning team scored."

"You wanna come back to Bear Cabin?" Julia asked in a soft voice. "Brenda might have something that'll make you feel better."

Yolanda glanced at Samuel, who was still staring at the marshmallow structure. He scrubbed a hand over his jaw and

61

let out a tired sigh. "Yeah, that sounds good," she said. Anything to get away from her giant stick-in-the-mud TB Buddy. A quick break from the Fox Cabin duo would help her get out of her head.

Chapter Six

Yolanda looked strange.

Samuel could guess why. When she and her friends, Julia, Brenda, and Sarah returned from Bear Cabin, they carried the faint scent of marijuana with them. The four women giggled their way through Joanne's explanation, missing most of the instructions for the Scavenger Hunt. This was a TB Buddy activity that would force them to work together right after a disastrous marshmallow building activity.

Yolanda didn't appear bothered... probably because she was high.

"Tell me what's happening?" she tried to whisper as some participants took off in different directions.

"As Joanne just explained: the people who won the last activity have a five-minute head-start. You and I will wait here with our clues until Craig blows the whistle. Now, can you stand up straight long enough?"

Yolanda's upturned face was as beautiful as it was petulant. "You sound irritated, Sam."

He didn't feel irritated... He felt something else entirely. She held on to his bicep to stay upright, but her gaze remained steady. He froze under her light touch, watching her fingers glide up to his shoulder. "No, I'm fine," he breathed.

"You say that often," she replied. "And I think you're lying every time."

"I have no reason to lie."

"Mmh." Her wry grin said that she didn't believe him.

He changed the subject. "So who was holding in Bear Cabin?"

"Why would I tell you?" she chuckled.

"I'm not a snitch."

She leaned against him, her breast brushed his arm. "If you can believe it, Brenda from Communications let us help ourselves to her stash," her voice dipped down to a whisper. "She has anxiety."

"I see," Samuel said, trying to ignore the touch of her soft bosom pressed against him and how it made him feel. He suddenly had the urge to touch all of her soft curves. "That was nice of her to share."

"I don't know how helpful I'm going to be on this journey," Yolanda admitted. "When I get high, I just feel like vegging out in front of the TV."

Her inability to take part in the latest TB Activity didn't really bother him. In fact, he didn't mind taking her by the hand and traipsing around Redstone Retreat. When it was just the two of them, Samuel could focus on Yolanda and shut everything else out.

* * *

Of course, they lost the Scavenger Hunt.

By the time it was over and done with, Samuel and Yolanda were the last TB Buddies to arrive back at the main lodge. At dinner that evening, she was ravenous. Samuel watched as she remained quiet long enough to scarf down baked chicken and mashed potatoes. Watching her eat... delighted him. Maybe it was because she was so quiet. He noticed she wasn't the only one; Sarah, Brenda, and Julia were also starving for carbs.

When Joanna came around with Daily Reflections, Samuel was curious to know what Yolanda would write. She was no longer high, but there was no telling what she might remember about their day together. Samuel wondered what he might put in his own reflection. He jotted down a few musings:

-I learned that my leadership style might not be effective

-I tend to rub people the wrong way with my blunt honesty

"What are you writing?" Yolanda asked him. She leaned over his shoulder as she sipped her water.

He shifted to cover his paper. "I wrote that my TB Buddy was too high to complete the scavenger hunt."

Her eyes widened in shock. "Oh my god, please don't write that," she whispered.

Yolanda's reaction made him grin. "I'm only joking," he whispered back.

She blew out a sigh as her shoulders sagged. "I hate it when you joke."

Samuel tilted his head as he regarded her. "I should try to come up with better material, I guess."

She propped her chin on her fist and smiled. "Just as long as you don't go to Peter for help..."

He gazed at Peter, who sat beside Julia, trying his best to chat her up. Julia wasn't responsive since she was still going to town on her mashed potatoes. "No, I better not."

"Are you disappointed that we lost out on the Target gift cards?" she asked in a soft voice.

Samuel shook his head. The Hedgehog Cabin made off with

65

two thirty-dollar gift cards after finishing the scavenger hunt first. "I'm disappointed about something else," he said, folding his paper.

Yolanda leaned closer. "What?"

Samuel had had a good deal to think about while he was dragging Yolanda all over the retreat grounds. When they arrived at the boathouse for their fourth clue, he realized there was something very wrong with their dynamic. He took the time to actually see her for the first time that day. As she stubbornly read the clue, while high, he realized that he'd behaved like a dick during the tower-building activity. What had changed from the previous night when they sat together joking around on her phone? He remembered feeling relaxed with her. Did the friction arise when they were thrown into group settings? He enjoyed being in charge, and the need to keep order felt even more intense. But being alone with her... things were different.

"I'm frustrated with myself for not letting you lead the group today," he admitted in a low voice. "There's no reason that activity couldn't have been... fun."

"It's killing you to say that word," she said with a sneaky grin.

He returned her smile as he ducked his head. "Would you like to go outside to talk? I feel like I might be better at this with privacy."

Yolanda nodded and stood from the table. "We're going to head out," she told the women and Peter.

Brenda gave her a thumbs up. "Sounds good. I'm going to get some more mac n' cheese," she said, taking her plate and standing.

"Grab me another cornbread muffin," Sarah said.

"Me too!" Julia chimed in.

Samuel guided Yolanda to the waste bins and plate station, suddenly aware of the itch in his palms. He didn't know where the sensation came from, only that his hands were now sweaty and a live-wire ran through his body.

Once outside, Yolanda took a deep breath and lifted her face to a starry sky. "It's beautiful out here," she said in a reverent voice. "And so quiet."

They walked away from the main lodge entrance and stopped along the path back to the cabins. It was the same spot where Yolanda had apologized to him the previous night. "I wanted to say something to you," he started.

"Let's sit on that stone bench over there," she suggested. "I want to see the lake at night."

The stone bench near the lake was a perfect place to rest after a large dinner. The space was lit by the same quaint lanterns that dotted the retreat. A pleasant breeze broke up the warm humidity, lifting the hairs on his arms and sending a chill down his back.

"Now what did you want to talk about?" she asked as shadows played across her face. An errant curl had escaped her high ponytail and settled against the back of her neck.

Samuel tried not to stare at it as he spoke. "I wanted to apologize to you," he said, angling his body towards her. They sat a few inches apart, not as close as last night. But he felt the magnetic pull from her all the same.

Yolanda drew one foot to the bench and hugged her knee to her chest. "Yeah?"

"I feel like we've started off on the wrong foot several times," he continued. "Not just here, but at work. I think some of that tension might be my fault."

Even in the shadows of the lantern light, her surprised

expression was still visible. "Yeah?"

"I'm kind of a stick-in-the-mud," Samuel admitted. "And it doesn't make me happy. In fact, I'm stressed out and anxious most of the time, like I'm performing day and night for a boss who… well, you saw Craig today. I don't think he takes himself too seriously," he paused when she giggled. "But when I look at someone like you: a brilliant professor, well-liked by colleagues and students… I get a little jealous."

"Of me?" she squeaked, gesturing to herself. "Messy me?"

"You're not that messy," he said with a smile.

Yolanda lightly shoved his shoulder. "Oh no, you don't have to lie."

"I'm not," he said. "You are someone I'd like to be more like."

After admitting that aloud, he held his breath and waited for her reaction. She scratched the back of her neck as she stared out over the lake. He wished he knew what she was thinking. Did he sound like a weirdo? "This makes so much sense," she said with a nod.

"It does?"

She turned towards him and grinned. "I guess I'm also a bit jealous of you, Sam. And my Leo pride makes it difficult to say it to your face, so I'm glad you said something."

She was jealous of him?

"You're so organized and precise," she went on. "Your life is so in order you have time to contribute to this journal or that edited volume. You're like a writing machine. I'm busy performing too, you know. Being this fun just requires a different labor."

Samuel sat back and considered her words. Maybe they were supposed to be TB Buddies. They both had something that the other wanted, and that mutual desire gave him his first spontaneous idea. "Can we try something? Together?" he asked.

"What?"

"If you help me learn how to relax, I'll help you get organized this semester. I can mentor you with the grant-writing if you'd like."

She nibbled on her bottom lip. The peek of her tongue was a delightful distraction that threatened to knock him off course. "That doesn't sound like a fair trade-off," she said.

Disappointment struck him hard. "No?"

She shifted on the bench to face him. "Teaching someone how to have fun for a few more days is relatively easier than grant-writing. I think you're going to work harder than I will."

Teaching her how to write a grant wouldn't be as laborious as she thought. Earlier in the day, near the boathouse, he decided that he liked Yolanda Watson very much. And the reason he didn't know how to act around her was because of his nerves, and their lack of communication. Perhaps if he was more honest about his feelings, they wouldn't have such a tense relationship. "I enjoy this stuff," he insisted. "Don't underestimate the pleasure you can get from formatting a document."

"But what about figuring out all those footnotes?" she teased in a husky voice.

He leaned forward, playing along. "We'd have to bridge the gap between MLA and Chicago."

Her arm brushed against his as she shifted closer. "I haven't worked with Chicago citation in years," she whispered. "Are you sure you can train a novice?"

Did she realize she was close enough to kiss? "Yes."

"Patiently?" she pressed with a smirk.

Samuel couldn't help himself. Once his gaze settled on her mouth, it lingered long enough to imagine his lips pressed against hers. He wondered what sounds Yolanda would make if he swiped his tongue against hers. Would she release a suffocated moan? Would her fingers toy at the hair at the nape of his neck? "I can be patient," he said in a low voice.

Heat replaced the dreamy look in her eyes. Yolanda's mouth parted, but no words came out. Instead, her eyes fell to his mouth.

He had only enough breath to utter her name. "Yolanda?"

Her tongue darted to the corner of her mouth as she placed a hand on his chest. "Would it be silly to start our relaxation lessons now?" she asked in a hushed voice.

She's touching me. She's touching me.

Surely this means something.

Her hand is on my chest.

She's touching me...

Could she feel his heart thumping wildly against his chest, desperate for her fingers to glide in any direction? The world slowed down to an excruciating pace as he watched her lean closer to his face. Their lips were only a breath apart. He froze, careful not to close the distance and frighten her off.

Yolanda flinched as something hit her on the side of the face. Her hand left his chest and began flapping around her head as she sprang from the bench. "It's on my face!" she screamed.

He couldn't see what was on her face because Yolanda was jumping around, frantically waving her arms. He had to assume it was a bug. "It's gone," he said, grabbing her by the shoulders and checking her over in the dark. "Yolanda, I don't see anything."

She could barely stay still in his grasp. "Oh my god, it flew right into my face! Did you see it? I think it was a grasshopper."

Oh boy... He now saw what attacked her. And it was trying to free itself from her thick, curly ponytail. Samuel guided her towards the nearest lantern. "Hold still while I get him out of your hair," he murmured.

Her body froze, but her arms had wrapped around his waist. "Please kill it," she said in a trembling voice.

"I'm not going to kill it," he told her. "Just hold still, and we'll get him hopping along." This was the second time Yolanda clung to him for safety... against an insect attack. Not that he minded. It wasn't often that he could come to a woman's rescue. The grasshopper twitched and fluttered in the tangle of her curls before Samuel could pluck him free. He tossed the critter into the grass and patted her on the back. "He's going back home to Mrs. Grasshopper," he whispered in her ear.

She had buried her face against his chest during the extraction. When she finally looked up, her cheeks were flushed with embarrassment. "I'm a city girl, remember?"

That much was clear, but he wouldn't chide her about it. Instead, he focused on her tight grip around his waist. She *could* release him, but she didn't. So he continued to rub her back, up and down, until her muscles relaxed. "Do you feel better?"

She gave a wordless nod, but hadn't released him.

"You were saying something before that grasshopper rudely interrupted us," he said in a soft voice.

Yolanda gave him a tremulous smile. "I was trying to kiss you," she admitted.

Her boldness shouldn't have shocked him. She routinely said what was on her mind. But his mouth went dry anyway. "Yeah?"

71

"I was flirting with you until it attacked me," she said in a serious voice. "The grasshopper ruined the moment."

Samuel swallowed. "Would it help if I hunt him down and kill him for you?"

Yolanda chuckled until her head hit his chest. "I should have asked before assuming you'd want to kiss me back," she said.

"The answer would have been yes."

They'd been holding each other for quite a while. He was reluctant to let her go after what she admitted. She wanted to kiss him. It had been a long time since he'd had a beautiful woman in his arms; he was unsure of what to do next. Let her go and quietly return to the cabin? Kiss her now, letting her know that he felt the same?

"Then we can wait," she said, pulling away from him. "We'll start having fun tomorrow. The indica strain makes me a little sleepy anyway."

Yes, he could wait.

Samuel had learned more than he had expected, beside Redstone Lake. The only thing that stopped Yolanda Watson from kissing him was an errant grasshopper. He would hold on to that knowledge as he slept. He grinned in the darkness as they walked back to Fox Cabin. A spring in his step and an excited thump of his heart propelled him forward.

Chapter Seven (Day 4: The Egg Drop)

She hadn't kissed him yet.

She went to sleep almost as soon as her head hit the pillow because the weed exhausted her. When they got ready the next morning, there were flirty smiles, but neither of them made a move. The friction that usually kept them at each other's necks was now replaced with a jittery sexual tension that made her giggle and him blush.

They ate breakfast with their usual group, pretending things hadn't changed the night before. Yolanda chatted with the people around her, but was hyper-aware of how close Samuel sat. Her body was in a perpetual state of flush when they brushed shoulders or caught one another's eye.

When they put their breakfast plates away, Yolanda pulled him aside. "Okay, TB Buddy, this is your first lesson."

Samuel was alert, looking around for a surprise attack. "What?"

She grinned. "Joanne is going to gather us up for another TB Activity and I want you to accept anything that she gives us. No matter how silly or embarrassing. Just go with it."

"What if it's another group thing?" he asked nervously.

"Same thing," she insisted. "You need to take a step back and not alienate your team members with rigid rules. Recognize the urge you have and consciously bury it."

His expression grew confused as he crossed his arms over his chest. Today's polo shirt was a powder-blue that looked lovely against his tanned skin. "It feels like I'd be burying a large portion of my personality."

Yolanda had to consider his words. "True, but you have to remember that this is a different rhetorical situation. In a silly team-building exercise, you're just trying to have fun... and part of that is fitting in with your audience."

He chewed on his bottom lip, which was really cute and distracting. Her eyes followed his movements as he pieced together her advice. "I don't have to smoke weed, do I?" he finally asked.

"Oh my god, of course not," she said with a startled laugh. "We're not complete teenagers. I'm not here to haze you."

He looked visibly relieved. *Jesus, is that what he thinks of me?*

"I'm just asking you to consider the feelings of the people around you," she explained. "Loosen up and be ready for possibilities."

Samuel nodded. "Possibilities..."

"Exactly."

His eyes fell to her mouth. "All possibilities?" The unmistakable heat in his forest-green eyes made her swallow. He was referring to something else, maybe their kiss, and the suggestion brought her right back to the heavy arousal she felt last night.

"Right," she whispered.

"I'm talking about a possible kiss," he said. "A bug interrupted us last night and I kinda want to explore that if you're willing."

She bit back a grin. "We need to work on your flirting skills," she said in a low voice.

He gave her a serious nod. "That's a part of my fun training?"

"Yes, but right now, we'll start with your autocratic tendencies in group settings. You don't always need to lead with a firm hand."

"Oh wow, Fox Cabin is having a secret meeting," Dean Craig asked as he sidled up beside them. "Scheming new ways to win TB Activities?"

Yolanda's heart jumped into her throat at the chance their boss had caught them flirting, but Craig was as oblivious as ever.

"Yes," Samuel said, saving her. "Yolanda and I are excited for whatever you and Joanne have planned."

Craig's smile grew as he glanced at Joanne, who was still eating breakfast. "I don't know what I would do without her," he murmured. "She's really the brains of the operation."

Yolanda and Samuel exchanged a secretive smirk. Their dean spoke as if they weren't even there. "Joanne is pretty great," she said.

Craig gave an absent nod. "She sure is...."

And without another word, their boss drifted away from them, towards Joanne's table. They watched him in wonderment before Samuel spoke in a low voice. "You see it, right?"

Yolanda nodded. "Craig's got it bad." When she looked back at Samuel, she noticed that his attention was no longer on Craig, but squarely on her mouth. She pursed her lips and swallowed. Yolanda didn't know if she'd ever get used to his intense gaze. His long dark lashes lowered slightly as his nostrils flared. "What?" she breathed.

The corner of his mouth quirked upward. "Just thinking about how my firm hand could be put to other uses," he whispered.

Yolanda's eyes widened in disbelief. "Are you flirting with me?" she asked.

"Too much?" his voice faltered with that same endearing blush. He raked his hands through his dark brown hair and shrugged his shoulders. "I rarely get the opportunity to flirt."

And yet, he managed that one line with enough sexual energy to catch her off guard. She shook her head. "No, that was great," she admitted, desperate to keep the huskiness from her voice. They didn't need to have such a heated moment near the cafeteria trash cans… They could save it for Fox Cabin. "Keep it up, TB Buddy."

A proud grin stretched over his face. "Thank you, TB Buddy."

* * *

The first TB Activity was a simple game of Two Truths, One Lie. Yolanda had played it dozens of times before with her own students as a first-day ice-breaker. She'd heard some pretty outlandish truths in her day as a facilitator and was interested in what adults would come up with. They all sat on the floor of Redstone Retreat's yoga studio in group circles. Her group included her TB Buddy, Julia, Brenda, Peter, and Chris. Samuel sat beside her, cross-legged and tense.

Yolanda had hoped that after their little talk, Samuel might be better at managing his group anxiety, but his body-language suggested he wasn't out of the woods just yet. "Who wants to go first?" she asked the group.

Chris from Communications raised his hand. "I can go." He looked at the ceiling and thought about his statements for a few seconds. "I can't eat eggs, I can't swim, and I can't speak another language."

"Oh, that's interesting..." Brenda intoned.

Yolanda tried to remember their breakfasts and wondered what Chris ate. "You *can* swim," she said.

He remained quiet so others could guess. When they all got the chance to figure out Chris's lie, he chuckled. "Brenda's the only one who got it. I never properly learned how to swim. Luckily, there won't be any water-related TB Activities."

"Those were good, Chris," Julia said. "What other language can you speak?"

He shrugged and ran a hand through his short blond hair. "I'm fluent in Russian. My grandmother was from a small Russian community in Estonia, and she taught me when I was a kid."

"Very cool," Peter said with a nod. "I guess I can go next?"

"Keep the jokes to a minimum," Julia warned.

While the rest of the group laughed, Peter cast Julia a sidelong glance and smirked. "I think you like my jokes, Julia."

The look they exchanged was brief and barely perceptible to others, but Yolanda caught it. There was a flash of softness in her friend's eyes that she'd never seen regarding Peter Leonard. Julia quickly rolled her eyes, but her brown cheeks darkened with embarrassment. "Get on with it," she said, waving her hand dismissively.

"Alright," he said, leaning back and pursing his lips. "I've climbed Denali, I've worked on an oil-rig in Alaska, and I had a pet snake when I was a kid."

Yolanda could believe the first two statements. Peter couldn't have been taller than six feet tall, but he had a solid and powerful build that could be useful for hard labor. He was only in his mid-forties, he could have done the oil work when he was younger. A pet snake was also possible, but she feared if he made a joke about Eden, they'd never be able to shut him up.

"You've never climbed Denali," Samuel said with a smile. "Or else we would have heard about it."

This garnered laughter from the rest of the group. "That's true," Chris said. "A mountain climber would never let you forget they'd tackled one of the Seven Summits."

After everyone guessed, Peter admitted that he'd never climbed Denali, but that he had lived in Alaska long enough to work on a rig with his uncle. "I wanted to be a herpetologist when I was a kid," he said. "I named my first boa Mike."

Yolanda let loose a full-body shudder and frowned. "Gross."

To her surprise, Samuel laid a large warm palm on her back. "I won't let the snakes get you," he said with a grin.

Before she could reply, Julia laughed. "So you've already discovered that she's afraid of all wildlife, Sam?"

His palm slid away from her back and returned to his lap. She immediately missed his touch, but was glad that no one seemed to notice the intimate display. "Yolanda's just a city-girl, that's all," he said.

She rolled her eyes at her group members. "Whatever…" she grumbled.

"I've seen you scream at a butterfly," Julia continued. "You claimed it was attacking you."

Yolanda scoffed. "It was fluttering its giant wings right in my face all threatening like this," she said, mimicking the movement with her hands in Julia's face. "Does that feel nice?"

"Bitch, your fingers in my face is not nice at all," her friend said, batting her hands away. "You almost killed an endangered monarch butterfly."

"How about I go next?" Samuel suggested.

"Go ahead, Sam," Peter said.

"I'm afraid of elevators; I took ballet lessons when I was younger, and I was born in Indiana." When he finished, Samuel had stumped everyone. His grin grew as the group members guessed, but he kept mum.

Yolanda didn't think anyone as stiff as Samuel could dance, but she'd also seen him make a leisurely exit from an elevator. She didn't believe he could be afraid of tight, enclosed spaces. "You were *not* born in Indiana," she said as the last person to guess.

As his eyes slid to her, his smile told her she'd guessed wrong.

"I'm fine with elevators," he said. "My mom ran a dance studio, and she taught me and my sister."

"Really?" Brenda said as she appraised Samuel's body with a dreamy expression.

Yolanda felt a small pang of jealousy watching her colleague openly ogling her TB Buddy and tried to dismiss it as quickly as possible. There was no need to be possessive of a man who wasn't her boyfriend.

"And I was born in Gary, Indiana," he added. "My dad worked in steel."

It surprised Yolanda to know he had come from a working-class family in the Rust Belt. But she had never asked, and he never spoke about his past. She didn't even know that he had a sister. She wondered what she was like and how old she was.

"How many years did you dance?" Chris asked.

Samuel shrugged. "I started when I was eight and, I don't know… I stopped some time in high school. It kind of got in the way of my studies."

"Very cool," Julia said, secretly nudging Yolanda. "So, Sam, you must be strong enough to toss women in the air, yeah?"

She shot her friend a pointed look. "It's not like cheerleading, Jules."

"No, it's not," he agreed. "But I can."

When she looked back at him, Samuel tried to maintain his smug grin even though his face grew redder by the second. Instead of reading into his words and his delicious grin, she took her turn. "I'll go next."

"Just don't lie about bugs," Chris said with a chuckle.

"I guess I can't since Julia already blew up my spot." The group settled down as she thought about her statements. She had been so focused on everyone else's turn, that she had neglected to think about a potential lie. "Okay… I didn't learn how to tie my shoes until I was ten-years-old. I'm the first teacher in my family, and I don't know how to whistle."

She bit back her smile as the group guessed. Peter couldn't believe the shoe-tying statement.

Samuel was the last person to guess, and he was correct. "You're *not* the first teacher in your family."

"Correct," she said. "That honor goes to my grandfather. He was a high school math teacher."

"Girl, you can't whistle?" Julia asked with a frown.

She shook her head. "Nope."

The group erupted into laughter, which led to a sidebar conversation that she knew would normally bother Samuel. When Yolanda glanced at him, to see if he had tensed again, she was surprised to find him staring at her.

His eyes flickered with mirth as he leaned close to her. "Would you like me to teach you how to whistle while we work on grants?" he whispered.

Her breath caught in her throat when she caught a whiff of his scent: a minty man's body wash and his aftershave. That he was close enough for her to feel the heat coming from his body, sent a shiver through her. "I don't want to add too many things to your already challenging job."

Samuel lowered his lashes slightly and replied, "It's no problem... After all, you just put your lips together and blow."

Yolanda's mouth fell open for the second time that day. She didn't know how she did it, but she had let loose a flirting monster in Samuel. Just giving him permission to be charming was enough to make him sound like a lothario. And she was excited to be on the receiving end of his attempts. "Sam..."

He sat back. "Too much?"

"What's too much?" Julia asked, bringing the group back together.

Yolanda blinked as she refocused her attention to the rest of the members. "Nothing, who wants to go next?"

Chapter Eight

Here's to having… fun.

Day Four's first activity became easier the more Samuel gave up control. He recognized how triggered he got when Julia veered them off course and distracted the rest of the group. But instead of getting annoyed, he took that opportunity to flirt with Yolanda. He would hold on to her reaction for a long time. Apparently, that retort was just as naughty as his "firm hand" comment. What's more was she liked it. Once Julia interrupted them, he watched Yolanda fluster through the rest of the game. He went back to being a professional, but the pleasure of catching the unflappable Yolanda Watson made him suppress a grin as the last two group members took their turn.

And now, they stood in the same field where the Human Knot game took place. Today's outdoor TB Activity was The Egg Drop relay race, and their teammates would be the same people from the last activity. The game would be based on speed and teamwork, something he didn't know if his team would be ready for.

"Okay, gang!" Craig announced. "The rules of The Egg Drop are simple enough. We have lanes set up for each group, with various obstacles blocking everyone's paths."

Joanne jumped in excitedly. "Each lane also has three white markings indicating every leg of the relay. Your team needs to decide which partners will start the race, who will be in the middle, and who will finish."

"Why do we need to have partners for this race?" Dennis from Philosophy asked.

"Well, that's the fun team-building part," Craig said in a voice normally reserved for something more exciting. *No, quit that.* Samuel stopped himself from being cynical and anxious about this. He was trying to have fun. "One TB Buddy will be blindfolded while the other guides them down the lane. So this exercise is as much about communication as it is speed."

"Aaaand whichever team gets an unbroken egg down their lane the fastest," Joanne interrupted, "will receive free campus parking for the semester!"

Free parking? That declaration earned Craig a whooping cheer from the participants. Professors had to pay for the privilege of driving to campus to the tune of $100 per month. Even Samuel felt a thrum of excitement. But after doing poorly for the last three TB Activities, he didn't have high hopes of winning today's event. And according to Yolanda, winning wasn't his primary goal. He just needed to lighten up and enjoy the rest of the week.

"Everyone take your blindfolds and spoons before positioning yourselves," Craig said, waving black strips of fabric in the air.

Yolanda sneaked a shy glance at him. "Who should go blind for this exercise?" she asked as Julia and Brenda collected their team's tools.

"Good question," he said. "I was going to ask which leg of relay we should do."

"Not the middle," she blurted.

Samuel raised a brow as he looked down at her. "Any reason?"

She ducked her face. "Middle of the road is boring."

Samuel "So, if you're not first, you're last?"

He loved the way she seemed to laugh with her entire body as she clutched his arm and her eyes squinted in the sun. His body didn't tense when she touched him; Samuel leaned into the warmth of her hand on his bicep. "Let's go last," she said, looking up at him with a wide grin. "I can wear the blindfold."

"Do you trust me to lead you?" Samuel asked.

Her eyes softened. "I think so... You won't let me trip over anything, will you?"

He shook his head. "Of course not, we'll go as slow as we can."

When the groups were in position with their spoons in hand and blindfolds covering their faces, Craig announced the last rule that would make their activity slightly more challenging. "Okay gang, so that this stays a communication challenge: you are *not* allowed to touch your TB Buddy. You must guide them verbally, but you *are* allowed to make the transfer from one egg carrier to the next. If your partner drops their egg, you must run back to Joanne for a new one. Everybody got it?"

"TB!"

"Great! Now put on your blindfolds and get your spoons ready!"

Samuel held Yolanda's spoon while she tied the black cloth over her face. The strip covered her eyes and the bridge of her nose. "Can you see anything?" he asked, waving a hand in front of her face.

She shook her head. "Nope," her hands extended before her. "Spoon?"

Samuel placed it in her grasp. "Got it?"

"Yes," she said with a smile. "Are you close by?" One hand was still extended towards him.

"I'm here." He stepped closer and allowed her to touch his chest. Her fingers lightly grazed against his pecs before finding his bicep. Just that brief touch made him press his lips together and bury a groan.

"On your marks, get set…" Joanne dragged out her pause. "Go!"

"We won't be able to touch when the egg gets to us," he reminded her.

"I know," she said in a low voice. "But for now, I need something to hold on to."

Samuel didn't mind being that something. He cherished every moment their bodies were near one another. Being so close to unraveling in her hands, losing his self-control, should have frightened him. Instead, Samuel felt emboldened.

"You should probably talk or something," Yolanda said, squeezing his arm. "I don't like the silence."

He noticed that about her. She could talk enough for both of them, but he didn't want to leave her hanging in this moment. "What would you like to talk about?" he asked.

Her lovely red lips pursed to one side of her mouth as she faced his general direction. "I want to know how you learned to be so slick overnight?"

Because she couldn't see him, he allowed a smile stretch over his face. He had hoped that his comments weren't completely ridiculous. Samuel's attempts with flirtation were off the cuff, and he was still quite self-conscious. "Slick?"

"'Put your lips together and blow?'"

"I like movie quotes," he replied, watching the race around

85

him. The team closest to Craig and Joanne had already dropped their egg during the first leg. The other team was slower than Peter and Chris, but not by much. "Did I do well?"

She nodded. "You can be very charming when you want to be. I hope you take this energy back to school this semester."

Yolanda's suggestion rang in his head. It wasn't a bad idea; he liked this light feeling in his chest. Could most days at Franklin University be like this? The promise of another smile in his direction, or a kiss, drove him mad with an excitement he hadn't felt in a long time. "Would you like to keep that energy with me?" he finally asked, watching her face.

Yolanda went quiet. Her mouth became a small "o" at his question, but her fingers tightened on his arm. "What are you asking?"

"Nothing too different from last night," he said. "We were going to kiss, possibly more... Do you think you'd still want to do that?"

The amount of seconds it took for her to answer was terrifying. How he now hung on her every word made him uncomfortable. It was as if he sought her approval in all things "fun." It was her sly grin that made him breathe easy. "I *did* promise you a kiss... I should probably make good on that."

"Only if you'd like to," Samuel said.

"I'd like to," Yolanda replied, squeezing his arm again. "If you're okay with it."

With her vision obscured, Samuel felt comfortable spilling some of his feelings. He still had time with Chris making the gentle hand-off to Julia. "I've wanted to talk to you for a while," he admitted in a low voice. "I was just afraid to get to know you. We've been at odds since last year... Kissing has felt like the furthest thing from my mind until now. But I *do* want that.

86

Does that sound silly?"

She shook her head. "No, it doesn't."

He sighed. "Well, that's how I feel."

"Thank you for trusting me with that information," Yolanda said as her hand slid down to his forearm. "I appreciate it, as your TB Buddy and colleague."

Samuel chuckled. "Thank you. Now, how do you feel as a regular woman who's not my TB Buddy?"

She joined in on his laughter. "Regular Yolanda would really like to make out with you like a teenager at summer camp," she lowered her voice, "I'd even let you get to third base."

He was glad she couldn't see him blush. "While I'm very excited to hear that, I need you to get ready for Julia."

Yolanda's body tensed. "Is she close?"

"Close enough," he said, pulling away from her grasp. "I'll help with the hand-off, but I need you to be calm, and follow my voice."

"Are we in the lead?"

Samuel thought twice before answering her. Yes, they were in the lead, but an overly competitive Yolanda didn't need to know that. "We're doing well," he said. "Don't worry about that."

She chuckled as she held her spoon aloft. "I really want that free parking spot."

"Would it help if I took your mind off the race?"

"Definitely," Yolanda said, nodding. "Keep being slick."

He watched Julia draw nearer to them and tried to suppress his laughter. "It's difficult to be slick on command, Yolanda."

"You work best when you're teasing me," she said.

Samuel moved closer to her ear. "I would imagine the teasing would make *you* more slick," he whispered.

Yolanda gasped. "Oh my god, you did it again." The unobscured parts of her face darkened with an embarrassed blush.

Sam delighted in seeing her bite her bottom lip and duck her head. "You have a point though," he said. "It works better when I feed off of you."

"It's good to know you're not averse to *feeding off me*," she said with a straight face. "I really enjoy it as a TB Activity."

For the first time since meeting Yolanda, Samuel let out an undignified snort of laughter. His face was on fire, but he still delighted in her ability to catch him off guard. "Team-building or third-base?"

"Pick one," she challenged.

"I'll think about that later, but for now, Julia's here with an egg."

"I'm ready," she said, jabbing her spoon in the air.

"Okay, we're here," Brenda said to Julia. "We're handing it off!"

"You guys better not fuck this up with your arguing," Julia said, holding the egg out.

"We're not arguing," Yolanda promised.

Samuel carefully plucked the egg from her spoon and transferred it to Yolanda's. "You've got the egg," he said. "And I'm right beside you; just follow my voice."

Yolanda held her spoon still and took her first steps forward. "Are we winning?" she asked in an excited voice.

"We're not going to focus on anyone else," Samuel replied. "We're just going to run our own race." He meant it. As much as he wanted to win free campus parking, this moment was more important. He wanted to work well with Yolanda, making up for all the other times they weren't on the same page.

Her nose scrunched. "You're not going to tell me who's in the lead?"

"Do you trust me?" he asked, following her timid steps forward.

"Is that from *Titanic*?"

"Maybe."

"Jesus..."

She set a good pace: not too slow and not fast enough to jostle the egg. Up ahead, a cardboard box obstructed their path. "In a few feet, I'll tell you to stop so we can get around the first obstacle."

"The box?" she asked.

"Yes, you're going to come to a gentle stop," he warned.

"Okay..."

"Stop," he said in a quiet voice.

She halted. "Where do you want me to go?"

"Take three small steps to your right."

Yolanda took three timid sidesteps until she cleared the box. Samuel stifled the urge to reach out and touch her, guide her through the course, keeping his hands by his sides.

"Now you can go forward," he said. "Keep the same steady pace. You're doing great."

"How are we doing?" she asked.

No one else captured his attention in that moment because Samuel's primary focus was the woman in front of him. Her half-shrouded face kept him so transfixed, he could ignore the busy race around them. "We're doing well, Yolanda, just focus on me and my voice."

A bright smile lit her face. "I will."

There was one last obstacle that blocked their path; a small fence that was about a foot from the ground. Yolanda couldn't sidestep this one, she'd have to go over it. "In about five feet, you need to stop again so you can step over a small fence."

"My arm is getting tired," she complained.

"You're almost there. Okay, gentle stop."

She paused just as the team beside them shouted: "Dammit!"

"Did someone drop an egg?" Yolanda asked.

Samuel laughed as he stepped over the short barrier. "I'm not paying attention to them," he said. "I only have eyes for you, Yolanda."

"The Leo in me loves hearing that," she said in a low voice. "You're probably looking at my tits."

He rolled his eyes. "I'm not focused on your... breasts."

"Shame," she sighed. "So, what should I do now?"

Samuel ran a hand over his mouth and thought about how to direct her without upsetting the egg. "Tap your toe against the barrier. Just see how high it is."

Yolanda lifted a leg, running her sneaker against the wooden fence. When her foot rested on the top, she pushed forward and straddled the obstruction.

"Slowly..." he warned.

After both feet were on the right side of the barrier, Yolanda faced the wrong way. "Now what?"

"Now turn ninety degrees to your left so you face the finish. You've only got a little more left, TB Buddy." Samuel finally glanced at the two other teams. He and Yolanda were in the lead! The first team's egg upset had slowed them down in the second leg, while the other team had just returned from Joanne with a fresh egg. He looked back at Yolanda, who was unaware of what was happening around her. "Easy does it."

"No more obstacles?" she asked.

"Nope, we're just walking now."

"Strolling?"

"It's a gentle promenade."

"I don't need to go faster?" Yolanda asked. "I feel like I should move faster."

"Not at all. The goal is just to finish without dropping the egg."

Yolanda frowned. "No, the goal is to finish *first* without dropping the egg."

Samuel stepped over the finished line and waited for her to follow him. "And you've done that," he said as soon as she walked across the threshold. "You can stop."

Yolanda froze in place with a huge grin on her face. "I did it?" she screeched.

"We're finished!" Samuel shouted. "Hearty TB!"

The rest of their team ran down the lane towards them as Craig and Joanne cheered. "Go Fox Cabin!"

Yolanda wrenched her blindfold from her face and looked at her egg. "Oh my god, we did it!" she screamed. "I can't believe we did it!"

Craig came jogging up to them to confirm their win. "Yolanda has a safe egg!" he called out to the others. He plucked it from her spoon and held it aloft like it was Excalibur. "We have a winner."

The other teams groaned in disappointment while giving a weak applause. Before Samuel could react, Yolanda jumped on him with a fierce hug. "Thank you," she whispered. "We actually worked together for once."

He caught her after a stumble and hugged her midsection. "Of course."

Over her shoulder, Samuel saw the rest of their team approach. Julia's grin paired with a curious expression as she watched their embrace. "Good job, you guys," she said. "You just saved me a couple hundred dollars this semester."

Yolanda released him, but kept one arm draped around him as she faced the team. "We all did this," she said. "You got it to us in no time at all."

Her arm wrapped around his middle, her fingers brushing against his ribs, branding his skin through his shirt. Clearly, she had no problem with this display of camaraderie in front of their colleagues. Was Samuel supposed to lean into her touch? Was he allowed to show how much he liked it?

He tried not to think; he just wanted to feel.

So he pulled her closer against his side and lifted his hand to his teammates for a round of high-fives. "Teamwork makes the dream work."

Chris and Peter were quick to reciprocate. "We're parking like kings this year!" Peter shouted.

Brenda hugged the other side of Samuel. "Thank you guys for keeping it together."

And for the first time since he began working at Franklin University, he felt like he belonged. The people whom he'd rushed past in the hallways were now congratulating him for the silliest competition that had nothing to do with research or teaching. It felt... nice.

* * *

Samuel tried to busy himself while Yolanda was in the bathroom. He heard water running when he fluffed his pillows and put his shoes by the door. Nervous energy coursed through his body as he contemplated how to approach her.

Continue being *slick*?

His nerves had plagued him all evening. While they ate dinner and gloated over their prize, he half listened to Yolanda recount how well he'd done to guide her. He was more focused on the brightness in her eyes as she laughed with the others. Yes, they had done a good job, but Samuel was more focused on making good on the flirting she'd chided him about. Every time she caught him staring at her, she'd throw him a wink before returning to the rest of the group.

Their walk back was quiet and awkward, as he had run out of things to say. His mind was on this moment, pacing the cabin, trying his best to relax. Yolanda would walk out of that bathroom soon, and he still didn't know how he would sweep her off her feet.

The bathroom door opened and she breezed out, shaking her curls around her shoulders. "Do you have anything to watch?" she asked. Her nightwear was a pair of pink shorts and a unicorn t-shirt that read: "EVERYBODY PRANCE NOW." She appeared relaxed enough as she flopped down on *his* bed.

He watched in stunned silence as she sat against *his* headboard and extended her legs against *his* bed spread. "I…"

"Or we can make out," she said with a playful grin. "I kinda promised you a kiss."

Samuel froze in place beside his dresser, forgetting how to walk all together. "Only if you, you know, if you want to," he stammered.

"It's not only if I want to," she said. "You'd have to want to as well."

He didn't know where his tongue went, so he nodded.

She curled her forefinger, beckoning him closer. "Good."

He walked forward, aware of every tense muscle in his body.

He hoped he wasn't sweating too much, that his hands weren't clammy, that he was a decent kisser. When he sat on the bed beside her, Samuel waited quietly for her to make a move.

"You're nervous," she said. It wasn't a question; she could just sense it.

"Kind of, yeah," he admitted. "My mouth might have signed some checks that I can't cash."

This made her laugh. Not in a mean way, but in that genial way that lured him closer to her. It was as if he was in on the joke, and not the butt of it. "I've never kissed a colleague before," she admitted. "But I feel good about this, Sam. I feel good about you."

He exhaled with relief. "Thanks for saying that. I thought I was supposed to be smoother than this."

Yolanda rested a hand on his forearm and smiled. "You've been smooth all day. I don't expect you to keep it up if it feels like work. Just relax."

Samuel took another deep breath and exhaled through his nose. "Okay."

"I'm going to kiss you," she said, shifting closer. The mattress dipped under her weight.

"Okay," he repeated. Their thighs touched the same way as the night they'd played around with Tinder.

She leaned forward, glancing from his eyes to his mouth. He fixed his gaze squarely on her lips. When she was just a few inches from his face, her pink tongue swept across her bottom lip. The sight made him clench the bedspread beneath him.

When their lips finally touched, Samuel let his eyes fall shut. The gentle pressure of her soft mouth pushed against him, tender at first, a little hesitant. Yolanda was testing the waters with a peck. Her gentle exploration was a delicate series of

94

feather-light kisses placed at the corner of his mouth and his bottom lip. He held absolutely still as her tongue swiped that same spot; he felt as though he was floating. The bed dipped again as she drew closer to him. Yolanda rested her hands on his chest and squeezed his muscles. Beneath her fingers, something twitched, making her grin against his lips.

When he opened his mouth, she immediately took advantage. She dipped her tongue inside and caressed his. Samuel let out an involuntary groan as she picked up the pace. He joined the party and slid against her as he cupped her face. He stroked her cheek with the pad of his thumb, letting his fingers brush the curls at her temple. He pulled her closer and coaxed her lips and jaw wider, deepening his kiss. When she gave a dreamy sigh against his mouth, Samuel savored the sound, placing it among her other sounds that pleased him.

Before he could push forward, Yolanda pulled back to look up at him. She pressed her fingers against her swollen lips with astonishment. "You're a really good kisser," she breathed. Her large brown eyes darkened as she glanced at his mouth. A dark blush settled in her cheeks as his fingers dug into her hair and softly cradled her neck.

"I'm glad to hear it," he said in a husky voice.

"I don't know what I expected," she admitted as she ran her hand down his chest. Every place her fingers touched left fire in their wake. His belly clenched as arousal shot through his body. "At first I thought we'd fumble around like a couple teens at summer camp. But I guess I've never done that, I've only seen it in the movies—"

"—Yolanda."

She paused. "Yes, Sam."

"Would you like to continue?" he asked, biting back a grin.

Yolanda gave a wordless nod.

Samuel took her by the hips and settled her on to his lap so she straddled his thighs. "By the way, you're a really good kisser too," he whispered.

Now that she was eye-level with him, she wrapped her arms around his shoulders and gave a shy smile. "Thank you."

He ran his hands up her back and groaned as she adjusted herself on his lap. The flimsy shorts she wore barely contained the heat between her legs as she pushed her hips against him. Samuel's body reacted upon seeing the flush in her face, the way her eyes fluttered closed. "Is this okay?" he asked.

She answered him with a devouring kiss that took him by surprise, but he quickly caught up to her. He was shocked at his own eager response to the touch of her lips, but recaptured her mouth, more demanding this time. She nipped at his bottom lip before licking away the sting. "You can touch me more," she whispered between kisses.

"Mmhmm," he mumbled against her mouth. In an instant, he ran his hands down her soft back to the curve of her ass, giving it an experimental squeeze. She felt lush in his hands, just as soft as he'd assumed. She ran her fingers through his hair, gently tugging at his scalp, sending a wave of pleasure to his cock. The pleasant floral scent of her hair brushed his face as he trailed slow kisses down her cheek to her neck. While holding her in place on his lap, Samuel slipped his hand under her shirt, tracing a path up her belly to her breast. Her nipples stiffened beneath his fingers.

She drew a sharp breath as she arched into his touch. "Yes."

Samuel fanned his fingers across the gentle curve of her breasts and squeezed. "This is okay?" he asked against her neck.

"More," Yolanda rasped.

He yanked down her bra cup and took her nipple between his thumb and forefinger, rolling the tight bud until Yolanda's hips swerved delicious circles against his erection. The sound of her desperate pants and whimpers filled the room, driving his need to hear more. Eager whimpers went into the Favorite Yolanda Sounds vault.

The sound he didn't expect to hear was a rapid knock against their door.

"Yolanda?" a woman's voice called out. "Are you busy?"

Yolanda froze in his arms. "Julia," she muttered.

Samuel reluctantly pulled his lips from her neck and slipped his hand out of her shirt. "You should see about her," he said in a strained voice.

"If we stay really quiet, she might go away," Yolanda whispered.

"Yolanda? Sam? Your lights are on."

She scrunched her face. "I'm coming! Give me a second..."

Samuel gave her a quick peck on the forehead. "I'll be in the bathroom."

She looked down at his groin and grimaced. "I'm sorry."

He shook his head. "Don't be," he chuckled as she stood from his lap.

Yolanda adjusted her bra and ran her fingers through her curls before running to the door. He made it to the bathroom just as Julia asked: "I'm not bothering you, am I?"

As he closed the door behind him, he rested his forehead against the smooth wood surface and blew out a frustrated sigh. His entire body burned with unspent desire. Samuel squeezed his eyes shut as he slipped his hand downward to his aching cock. Before tugging his release, he quickly turned on the shower behind him. While he stripped off his clothes, he convinced himself that he could do the one thing he was good at: remain in control.

Chapter Nine (Day 5: Spirit Hike)

Okay, so they'd kissed.

And it was amazing.

At least it was before Julia broke up the party. Before Yolanda could catch her breath and digest the fact that her (former) nemesis' fingers stroked her aching nipples until a whimper spilled from lips, she had to see to her friend.

Julia had something quite surprising to reveal to her.

She and Peter Leonard, joke-telling theologian and former oil-rig worker, kissed by the lake, under the moonlight. According to Julia, who looked wild-eyed by the whole affair, *she* made the first move and she didn't hate it. In fact, she wanted to do it again. Soon. They huddled outside of the cabin and spoke in low voices while Samuel disappeared into the bathroom. Yolanda could only imagine what he was doing in there, but Julia hadn't even asked about her missing TB Buddy.

"What are you doing here? Asking me for permission?" Yolanda asked.

Julia pulled her cardigan up to her ears and looked around the darkness before whispering, "I need my best friend to tell me if I'm making a mistake."

She *definitely* was not in a position to tell her friend about mistakes. She had just finished riding her own colleague's lap like he was a rodeo bull. And gauging what was beneath his khakis, the estimate wasn't too far off. "We know Peter; he's kind, smart, and *sorta* funny. It sounds like he really likes you. I don't think he would hurt you."

"Yeah, but office romances are complicated," Julia said around the thumbnail she bit. "What if we have to break up? He's in the office right next to mine."

Yolanda's face was on fire. Her friend had pointed out the one concern she'd tried to ignore while tangled in Samuel's arms. "Why did you kiss him?"

Julia shrugged. "Because I wanted to? I don't know if it's this damn retreat, and the fact that we're all stuck with each other, but maybe I noticed something different about him. Maybe he's not *just* corny-Peter."

"Really?"

Her friend nodded. "It felt... great. He's got really strong hands and when they're pressed against me, I just lose my head."

Yolanda's eyes widened as she listened to Julia. "Oh my god, Jules."

"Sorry," she said, leaning against the doorjamb. "I must sound ridiculous right now. Especially after I tried to shove you into Sam's arms."

"No, no, absolutely not," she said, pulling Julia into an embrace. "You're not ridiculous at all. It was probably all of that oil-rig talk. You've always gone for the brawny manual laborer type."

In that moment, she struggled over what to tell her friend. Perhaps it would have been comforting for her to admit she was also getting entangled. But the thing Julia said about complicated office-romances rang loudly in her ears.

"I think you should do what feels good," Yolanda said. "I

know you'd tell me the same, right?"

Julia pulled back slightly and peered at her. "I would..." she said with a note of suspicion. "You don't think it's a bad idea?"

Yolanda let out a halted laugh. "You're both consenting adults who are, you know, team-building. I don't think it's a bad idea."

Julia gave a slow nod. "Okay. Because I want to do it again."

Yolanda squeezed her friend tightly. "I'm happy for you, Jules."

And that was the first time she had ever lied to her best friend.

It was the morning after and Yolanda still didn't know why she'd done it. But as she stared at Samuel, who stood with a crowd of professors outside of the main lodge, she felt an awful pit in her stomach. After breakfast, they took part in another TB Activity, The Blind Draw. She and Samuel sat back-to-back, describing images that the other had to draw based on verbal command. Both of their pictures came out like shit because Yolanda got distracted while giving directions and barely listened while Samuel guided her. She was too busy thinking of worst-case scenarios.

This afternoon's group TB Activity was a required Spiritual Hike through the woods using the TB Buddy system. The "spiritual" part was up to the individual hiker, as per HR policy. While she hung out on the outside of the large group, Samuel hadn't noticed her absence. He was slowly becoming a little social butterfly, chatting with Chris, Brenda, Peter, and Julia. At one point, Samuel doubled over with laughter at something Peter said. Yolanda was proud of him. Day-Five-Samuel was quite different from Pre-Team-Building-Samuel, and she felt responsible for the transformation.

But the pride was short-lived as she worried the zipper on her fanny-pack. Making out with Samuel was nothing short of amazing, and like Julia, she wanted to do it again and again. But at no time did she and Samuel ever discuss the consequences. She was surprised that a man who was a stickler for the rules had expressed no objections. After Julia left and she returned to her bed, Samuel asked her if she would like to join him for an episode of *House M.D.* on his bed. It was cute, and she readily accepted, climbing into bed with him and snuggling against his chest. They had cuddled and watched Dr. Gregory House abuse his employees in the same bed.

Nothing spicier than that. They simply watched television and talked about their lives. He told her more about his parents, who had recently moved to a suburb outside of Gary, Indiana. His younger sister was a lawyer who lived in New Jersey with her husband of ten years. She told him about her family, who lived in Central Illinois. They both described their graduate school and job search experience. She learned that they had both worked hard to get where they were. Only Samuel was still working, while Yolanda took a well-deserved rest on her laurels. After that conversation, she felt as though she understood him better, but their talk didn't ease her nerves.

He was still her colleague, and they were still going to fuck.

"Does everyone have a bottle of water?" Craig asked the crowd.

"TB!" It was funny how acclimated they'd gotten to saying that nonsense, but Yolanda mumbled along all the same.

Samuel left his small group to approach her. "What are you up to over here?"

"Just thinking," she replied with a strained smile. She was getting used to seeing his beautiful smiling eyes peer down at her. When she stared at them, she couldn't forget how heated their make-out session got. How she felt in his hands and against his skillful lips. Yolanda wondered what else he could do with that sensuous mouth.

Samuel hitched his backpack forward and narrowed his eyes. "I can see it on your face."

Is it that obvious?

Yolanda's cheeks burned at his teasing accusation. "Are you ready for a hike today?" she asked, changing the subject.

"No," he said. "I would rather be in the cabin instead."

She chuckled. "Working on your syllabus?"

Her laughter died the moment she saw his expression. His eyes darkened despite the bright sunlight as he licked his lips. "No," he said resolutely.

"Oh…"

"I keep thinking about what would have happened if we weren't interrupted," he said, standing close and speaking softly. "Have you thought about it?"

"Yes." She started thinking about it after they'd woken up in the same bed and began getting ready for the day. He put on today's polo shirt: yellow, while she slipped on her sneakers thinking about the throb between her thighs and who put it there. When they sat back-to-back talking and drawing, his warmth spread throughout her body and settled in her womb. After spending four days with him, Samuel was quickly burrowing himself into her brain. "I can't stop thinking about it."

"Maybe we can pick up where we left off tonight?" he suggested in a light tone.

His forced nonchalance was enough to make her grin, then laugh. He was just as nervous as she was, which relieved her. "I'd like that," Yolanda said without thinking. How could she have hated this man?

"Alright now," said a grizzled voice in the crowd. It was Gus Kelly, owner of Redstone Retreat, making an announcement. "I heard you all have a hike that will take most of the day. I suspect you'll make it back just before dusk, so we'll probably have dinner ready for ya. I want to remind you folks to stay with your partners while you walk the woods and stick to the Maple Paths. The incline ain't enough to call home about, and you're not gonna do any serious climbing. This is a tennis shoe kinda hike if you catch my meaning. My chief concern is that you bring a bottle of water with you, and if you're snacking, don't litter. Any questions?"

No one said a word. Yolanda was too focused on her thoughts to bother Old Gus. Perhaps she needed a long puritanical hike to clear her mind of Samuel. As she gripped her water bottle in one hand, she marched forward.

Samuel marched by her side, his yellow polo shirt a clear beacon in her brain fog.

* * *

Yolanda was irritated that she'd drank most of her water on the first leg of the hike and now she had to pee. As a city girl, she'd never had to pee in the woods and wasn't excited about starting at thirty-eight years old. If she could just pick up the pace, she could make it back to the lodge before squatting behind a bush.

But she really needed to go.

She looked up to the cloudy sky, half shrouded by the thick forest canopy, and let out a tired sigh. If it started raining, the urge to relieve herself would be the only thing she'd think about.

"You wanna take another rest?" Samuel asked. Even though they trailed further behind the others, he was still concerned about her comfort. His question bloomed within her chest, making her reconsider her ban on peeing in the forest.

"If you don't mind…" she said, holding up her nearly empty water bottle. "I kinda need to use the bathroom."

Samuel stopped short. "Sure, let's take a break here."

The last hiker turned the bend up ahead, leaving them to a quiet forest. "You're not afraid of getting left behind?"

He shook his head. "Gus said to keep to the trail and we'll get back without a problem. It doesn't matter to me when we get back."

Yolanda smiled. "Thanks, Sam." She peered around the thick brush of the woods and wondered where, off the beaten track, was the best place to squat. She didn't want to do it anywhere near Sam. "I'm just going to go out a few yards, okay?"

He stuffed his hands in his pocket and turned his back to her. "Just don't get lost on me."

"Okay," she said, creeping off the path. The forest floor was littered with dead logs, giving shelter to moss and mushrooms. Thin sapling branches jutted from all directions, scratching her legs as she took hesitant steps forward. One wrong step on an uneven rock or a root and Yolanda could turn an ankle. She was also careful not to touch any of the dense greenery that came to her hips. She couldn't tell the difference between oak leaves and poison ivy.

A few yards into the forest, she looked over her shoulder for Samuel, who stood in the same spot she left him. Pine branches now obscured her from his vision. At least she hoped. She had wanted to find a nice little spot behind a tall bush, but poking gnarls of vegetation filled all the spacious forest bathrooms. "Team," she called out.

"Building," Sam replied in a loud voice.

If she could still hear him, maybe she could go a little deeper into the woods. A couple yards ahead sat a bush that looked promising. She minced toward it, keeping her hands and arms away from the plants she couldn't identify. "Team!"

"Building," he shouted.

Yolanda quickly undid her denim shorts and took stock of the surrounding thicket. She didn't find evidence of snakes or spiders as she kicked at the dirt. She shoved her shorts and underwear down as she squatted, willing her bladder to empty as quickly as possible. While she went, Yolanda fumbled around her fanny-pack for fast food napkins she took with her. Afterwards, she adjusted her clothing and rinsed her hands off with the rest of her water. "Team," she called out.

"Building."

Yolanda was about to walk back towards Samuel, but she heard something in the quiet forest. Something aside from the chatter of birds above her. A snuffling noise. She turned around to find the source, and at first, couldn't see anything in the greenery.

But then she heard it again.

A low grunt or sniff to her right.

Every muscle in her body tensed as she trained her eyes on a thick copse of trees just ahead of her. When a large black mass moved, she let out an involuntary squeak before slapping her hand over her mouth. It ambled slowly, but it eventually revealed itself.

A goddamn bear.

Was she surprised that this was happening to her? Of course

not. If anyone was going to have a bear encounter on this trip, it would be the self-proclaimed city girl. While she stood utterly still, the black bear continued moving. It was about thirty feet from her, nosing around on the forest floor. Hopefully looking for nuts and berries. Black bears don't normally crave human flesh. But it would be just like Yolanda to run into Wisconsin's only man-eating bear… It appeared to be alone, which might be good? If cute little cubs were involved, the situation might have been bad.

But it was already looking bad.

And it was getting worse.

Just as Yolanda took a step backwards, the most cliche thing happened. She snapped a dead branch with her sneaker, causing the man-eating bear to lift its head. "Oh god, no," she whispered.

They had locked eyes, she and the bear. She searched her mind for any meaningful wildlife knowledge. *Are you supposed to run? Or should you curl into a ball and wait for the bear to roll you about?*

"Team!" Samuel called out.

She jumped at the sound, keeping her eyes on the bear, who now seemed interested in their situation. For the first time in a really long time, Yolanda Watson was speechless.

"Yolanda?" Samuel's voice sounded so far away, but he was her only means of safety.

It was as if the bear knew that, because he shuffled forward, closing the gap between them by about ten feet. At this distance, she understood the full scope of how much trouble she was in. It was slightly bigger than the bears she'd seen in news reports. The cute kind that ended up in backyard swimming pools. She assumed it was a male bear, a loner who hunted unsuspecting

Black women.

"Yolanda, are you okay?" Samuel's voice was getting closer.

"Bear," she said in a shaky voice. "There's a bear, Sam."

Behind her, she could hear his footsteps breaking through the brush. "There's a what?" he asked.

As if to announce itself, the bear let out a loud grunt as he lifted his head and sniffed the air.

"Oh my god, it can smell us," Yolanda muttered.

"What are you saying?" Just as Samuel arrived at her side, the bear got more curious and ambled closer to them. "Oh, shit!" He stopped short and flung a protective arm over her chest. "It's a bear."

"Exactly," she breathed. "What do we do?"

"Uh…" Samuel's face was whiter and sweatier than usual as he stared the bear down. The distance between them and it had narrowed to about ten feet. "We've gotta make ourselves appear large and threatening. Starting waving your arms and shouting."

"When can we run?" Yolanda asked.

"You can't outrun a bear," he said, waving his arms.

She quickly followed his lead. "Get!" she shouted in her loud professor voice. "Get going, bear! We don't want you! Can't you see we don't want you here!"

"Haarrgh! Shoo now! Get!"

Between the two of them shouting, the beast looked confused. It took a tentative step forward, but paused when Yolanda started jumping up and down. "Get away, bear!"

Samuel stood taller than she, and probably made a more intimidating meal, but the bear still focused on her. "Go'n and get now," he snarled, taking a brave step towards the animal. "Get out of here!"

The predator stopped in his tracks, which was great... but when it tipped its body back to stand on its hind-legs, Yolanda screamed. The bear was much taller than she expected. "When do we run?" she asked again.

"WE DON'T!"

I don't want to die like this. I don't want to die like this. I don't want to—

"Keep waving your arms," Samuel reminded her.

Yolanda went back to waving her arms like a loon and shouted: "I don't want to die in Wisconsin! Don't kill me during a team-building retreat! I have a life in Chicagoooo..."

Her admission seemed to sway the bear's murderous intent. It dropped on all fours and gave a disgusted snuffle. They continued shouting at it until the animal flipped its head in a strangely irritated manner. As though *they* were taking up too much of the bear's time. Finally, it turned tail and wandered away, leaving them frightened and relieved.

For a few minutes of painful silence, they watched the bear disappear into the forest. Yolanda's heart rate was shattered and she could barely keep her breathing under control. Her hands shook like leaves in the wind as they hung by her sides.

Sam made the first sound, his shoes crunching against branches. He turned to her and said in a quiet voice, "Now we run."

That was all Yolanda needed to hear as she tore off in the opposite direction. Sam was hot on her heels as they traversed the woods. Within minutes, her feet landed on the soft springy pine needles of a narrow trail, hopefully leading to safety.

But she didn't stop there.

Adrenaline pushed her forward, faster than she'd ever ran in her life. And she *hated* running. She heard Sam's panting behind her and only checked once to see if he was near. He was. Yolanda didn't stop running until she saw the clearing for Redstone Retreat in the near-distance. When she skidded to a stop, she doubled over at the waist and planted her hands on her knees.

"Oh, lord," she muttered as blood rushed to her head. "Oh, lord…"

Sam laid a hand on her back, making her jump with a yelp. "I'm sorry," he panted. "But we gotta keep going. We're almost there."

Together, they hurried towards the retreat, towards safety, and Yolanda was thankful for the firm hand resting against her sweating back.

Chapter Ten

Samuel was damn near ready to collapse when they made it back to the main lodge. The professors were standing around outside, not paying attention to the exhausted buddies who approached. "We're back," he croaked as they stumbled towards the crowd. Julia was the first to notice them.

"Where the hell have you two been?" she demanded. "And why does it look like Yolanda's been running? She never runs."

"There... was... a bear," Yolanda said through shallow pants.

And that was the last thing she said, because she promptly fell against Sam. He caught her before she hit the ground, but the awkward catch sent them both to the dirt.

Julia and Peter both ran up to them; Craig was not too far behind, and Joanne huffed towards the small circle forming around them. "Oh my god, what happened to her?" Julia shouted.

Samuel tried to cradle her upper body, but her dead weight made it difficult to get a grip on her. "We ran into a black bear, off-trail," he said. "But we scared it off."

"We were about to send a search party for you two," Craig said, assisting Samuel and Peter in picking Yolanda up. Once the men got her on her feet, Samuel hoisted her up in his arms. "Do we need to take her to the medical center?"

Samuel shook his head. "I'm taking her back to the cabin."

"I'm coming with you," Julia said as she followed Samuel.

"You're a good TB Buddy, Sam," Joanna said in a trembling voice. "I'm so thankful that Yolanda had you out there."

He was also thankful to be with her. There was no telling what would have happened, but he knew that they *both* needed to scare the bear off. Together. As they trudged away from the murmuring crowd, Julia asked in a soft voice, "Is she going to be okay?"

The look of concern in her dark eyes almost made Samuel falter because he imagined it looked quite similar to his own. Julia loved her friend dearly, and he was grateful to bring Yolanda back to the retreat in one piece. "She'll be fine," he assured. "She had the fright of her life and then ran like hell to get away. She's in shock and exhausted. But when she wakes up, she'll be happy to see your face."

Julia rummaged around Yolanda's fanny pack for the cabin keys and let them in. Inside, Samuel laid her on her bed. He kneeled beside the bed and gazed down on her. Julia sat beside her and smoothed frizzy curls out of Yolanda's face. "I know my city girl freaked the fuck out," Julia chuckled softly.

Samuel laid the back of his hand on her sweaty forehead. She was a little warm, but that wasn't alarming. "Honestly, we both did. My brain stopped working for a second before we started screaming at it."

"Was it huge?"

"I'd say it was a full-grown male."

"It was a massive… man-eater," Yolanda murmured with her eyes still closed.

Julia leaned down to cup her friend's cheek. "Hey girl, are you feeling okay?"

Yolanda cracked her eyes. "Tell Craig that if he sends me into the woods again, I'll quit. Fuck tenure and the job market."

Julia glanced at Samuel with a wobbly smile. "She's good."

Yolanda's gaze slid to Samuel as well. "Thank you for saving me," she whispered.

Without thinking, he took her hand and brought it to his lips. "I wasn't going to let you fight a bear by yourself," he said, kissing her knuckles.

Yolanda froze, casting a nervous glance at Julia, who now regarded them with a curious expression. "Okay, Sam... Yolanda. What's going on here?"

Samuel was hesitant to release her hand. If there was anyone who might understand this newfound relationship, it might be the woman who was secretly making eyes at Peter Leonard. "Yolanda has been teaching me how to loosen up," he said carefully.

Julia's mouth quirked. "Loosen up?" she asked.

"Jules," Yolanda started.

"No, I get it," her friend chuckled as she stared at Yolanda. "When were you going to say something?"

With their hands still joined, Yolanda looked bashful. "I just wanted to talk about how you were feeling last night."

"Girl, please... You were being shady."

"Do you forgive me?"

"Of course I do," Julia looked at their joined hands. "So this is a thing? My Sam and my Yolanda, sitting in a tree?"

"Not today," Sam quipped. "Bears climb trees really well."

His remark earned him eye rolls from both women.

"But yes," he added. "If Yolanda doesn't mind me taking my loose version back to Chicago, I'd like for this to continue being a thing."

Yolanda was quiet for a moment, which was a feat for her. He held his breath because being vulnerable in front of her *and* her best friend was a nightmare. This level of transparency was new and quite uncomfortable. Finally, she smiled brightly. It was *that* smile he was getting used to; the kind that made her eyes squint with joy. "I'd like this to be a thing too."

"Oh, the romantic overtures," Julia said sarcastically. "Shakespeare would be so proud of you guys."

Yolanda pulled herself up in bed, resting her back against the headboard. "Okay, you got jokes? Have you talked to Peter about *your* thing?"

Her friend pursed her lips and narrowed her eyes. "Things were discussed on the trail."

"Maybe you oughta find him and discuss more things. I'd like to talk to Sam a little more."

Julia threw up her hands and stood from the bed. "Right, right, I know when I've overstayed my welcome," she said moving towards the door. "I'll tell the rest of the gang you're okay... and that you're not suing Franklin U?"

Yolanda shook her head. "I haven't decided just yet."

"Fair enough," Julia replied as she closed the door behind her.

When they were alone, her attention settled on to him and he drank it in. Seeing her dark eyes flutter at him was his reward for scaring off a bear. Samuel gripped her hand tighter and admitted, "I've never been so scared in my life."

"Me neither," she said. Yolanda pulled him towards her and cupped his cheek. "I think after a near-death experience, we deserve to know what happens to us now."

"These high-stress situations aren't good for relationships. Look at Sandra Bullock and Keanu Reeves," he joked. "He didn't even make it to *Speed 2*."

She smiled. "I don't want to sound arrogant, but maybe it could work for *us?*"

He drew closer to her face, focused on her lush lips. "Yes, it could," he whispered. "We could be different."

She took him by the neck and pulled him the rest of the way. When their lips met, Samuel felt the thrill of a thousand missed kisses pent up and longing to be released. Their tongues met and mingled, doing a dance that was familiar, yet seeking new heights of pleasure. He groaned against her mouth and she answered by nipping at his bottom lip. As their kiss deepened, he climbed on to her bed, on top of her, caging her body beneath his. He stroked her hair away from her sweaty temple before tracing a path of kisses down her neck. Samuel needed to pick up where he left off last night, before Julia interrupted them. He needed to feel all of her.

As his hands slipped under her t-shirt, she arched away from the bed. Quick to meet his touch. When she broke away, she let out a harsh breath. "Please, Sam. Can we do something more?"

"Of course," he said, setting a familiar trail of kisses down her neck. "We can do whatever you want."

"Touch me."

He could do that. He started by pulling her shirt up over her chest, revealing her light-pink bra. She assisted by reaching around and pulling the straps down and unhooking the back, letting her breasts free. He was met with beautiful brown mounds of soft flesh, tempting him to squeeze and caress. Her dark brown nipples were already stiff, ready for licking. Samuel took a deep breath and fanned his fingers across one, marveling at Yolanda's response to his touch. She let out a satisfied moan and sank against her pillows.

It wasn't fair for her to be the only one topless, so he quickly pulled his polo over his head and flung it on the floor; messy floor be damned. "You're so beautiful, Yolanda," he breathed against her skin, before latching onto her nipple. He sucked deep, feeling her writhe beneath him. As he swirled his tongue around her, he clutched her hips and tried undoing her shorts. Again, his TB Buddy was enthusiastic in assisting him with her undressing. Yolanda did most of the work, shoving her shorts and panties down her thighs and onto the floor. "Do you mind?" he asked as his hand trailed down her belly towards her pussy.

"God, no," she said in a harsh breath and widened her legs.

When he released one nipple, he stroked and teased until his mouth found the other. Yolanda's fingers were in his hair, guiding and holding him in place. This was where he belonged. As his other hands brushed the soft curls of her mound, her breath quickened and her hips bucked under his gentle exploration. She was already damp and hot under his palm, his fingers sliding easily through her folds. The silken flesh lit a fire in him and burned brighter as he stroked with one finger and then two. Samuel released her breasts to watch her reaction while he touched everything but her clit.

Yolanda's lips pressed together in a thin line as she arched her back and widened her thighs. A blush that started at her chest had drifted up her neck and settled into her cheeks, creating a beautiful wanton vixen he'd never seen. She could be sly and coy, or she could be charming and mischievous, but Samuel had never seen her completely undone and wanting more.

He wanted to give her more.

Samuel had set his mind to pleasing her, giving her what she needed, and like all worthwhile goals: he wanted to do this perfectly. He wanted his touch to be the only touch Yolanda would need. And if he couldn't do it right the first time, he wanted to try again until he got it right. He could be her perfect Virgo.

"Sam," she panted. "More."

He slid his fingers up and down, coating them in her juices, before finally touching her clit. It was as though a bolt of lightning struck her by the way her hips bucked against the mattress. Soon she rode against him, reaching for his next stroke. Samuel stared down at her face while she watched his hand work steadily against her pussy. She moaned and thrashed her head against her pillow until she gripped his wrist and breathed hard, "Inside me."

Samuel followed her instructions, inserting his middle finger into her wet tightness. Her whimpers became muffled cries behind her fist as she rode his hand. He rocked against her hip at the same rhythm, grinding his aching erection against her hips. He tried not to think about coming undone; he wanted to remain in the moment like she had wanted. For there was no other woman he wanted to be loose with, to break free from the chains of decorum and neatness.

"Another finger," Yolanda ground out. Her eyes squeezed shut as she lifted from the bed. "Keep touching my clit."

Samuel did as she said while kissing her neck, the top of her chest, and then her breasts. He tried to pepper as much of her body with kisses as he could. Her wetness coated his fingers until all he heard in their cabin were the sounds of his hard breathing, her guttural moans, and flesh slapping flesh. He kept rhythm until Yolanda lurched forward and clamped her thighs around his hand.

She muffled her cries in the crook of his neck as her body wracked with tremors. From inside of her, Samuel felt her walls flutter then squeeze in spasms. "Omigod, omigod," she breathed against his chest. It took a moment for her muscles to loosen and her breathing to return to normal. Yolanda ran her nails up his chest, lightly scratching his nipple as she went. Samuel's breath hitched as her fingers trailed along his jaw before touching his bottom lip. She leaned forward and kissed him there. "Thank you for that," she whispered.

"You're so beautiful stretched out like this," he murmured against her lips. "I just want to touch you everywhere."

"Yeah, well, touching my favorite place was an excellent start," she said through a tired chuckle.

Samuel reluctantly pulled his hand away and adjusted his uncomfortable erection. "Happy to start there," he said. When he tilted her head back and smooth her hair from her face, she presented him with a languid smile. "What do you think? Should we try that again some day?"

Her brow furrowed. "You make it sound like a long time from now. We could do that again tonight, tomorrow, and the next day. I'd love to return the favor, you know."

Samuel liked how her mind worked. "I'm just taking the temperature of the situation."

She nodded at his hand. "Is that what you're calling it?"

He let out a choked laugh. "Okay, okay..." he said, lying beside her. "This is new for the both of us and I just want to be careful."

"I'm tempted to say that's Virgo-Sam talking," Yolanda said, resting her head on his chest. "But I guess there's no need to rush anything, right?"

"No," he said, shaking his head. "I'm right here."

"That sounds lovely," she replied earnestly.

A text notification pinged from the floor. Her phone, no

doubt. "You wanna get that," he said, stifling a yawn.

"No, it's probably just Richard..."

A smug grin stretched over his face. "Fuck Richard."

Yolanda gasped. "Samuel Morris, I've never heard you curse!"

He shrugged. "I'm trying it out. You've still got Fun n' Loose Sam for a couple more days."

She snuggled closer to him, rubbing her legs against his. "I've created a monster."

As he gazed down the length of her nude body stretched beside his, Samuel took in the curve of her dimpled thighs and the slope of her generous hips. He couldn't believe his luck. Monster or not, he didn't mind being a little bad.

Chapter Eleven (Day 6: Free Day)

Finally, a day that had not been planned by Craig and Joanne.

Their last day of the retreat was considered a "Free Day," with no scheduled competitions. The next day, they would pack their things and head back to Chicago, with a week left before school started. Yolanda reluctantly spent the day in Bear Cabin with Julia, Brenda, and Sarah, working on her syllabus. She would have rather spent it in bed with Sam, but he convinced her that work was a good thing. The kiss he gave her before she left made her swoon *and* curse his work ethic.

When she saw Sam next, it was at the Last Night Bonfire, a TB Activity closely supervised by Gus Kelly and another Redstone employee. That evening's dinner was being grilled up by the kitchen staff while Franklin U's faculty was in charge of their own s'mores.

As Yolanda waited in line for a hot dog, she felt a warm hand rest on the small of her back. "I love the feeling of finishing a syllabus," Samuel whispered. "The sense of completion is something else."

Samuel was still going to be Samuel.

"I usually feel a mixture of relief and guilt," she admitted. While she hadn't received complaints from her students regarding her lateness, she still felt guilty about not giving them an immediate plan for the semester.

His hand slid up her back and rested on her shoulder. "If you ever want to work on syllabi together..."

Yolanda leaned into his embrace and chuckled. "You'd be proud to know that I finished one with the ladies in Bear Cabin. Only two more to go."

Samuel gasped. "And no one got high?"

She retrieved a plate and a hot dog bun before scoffing. "We did not get high. We worked on class prep and gossiped. It was a drug-free cabin today."

"Gossiped?"

"Yeah." She stepped up to the grill-master. "Can I please have a kielbasa?" The cook dropped a sausage into her open bun while Samuel stood beside her. She left him behind for the condiment station, wondering what made him pause. Was he worried about what they said in Bear Cabin? She waited for him to eventually speak as she loaded her sausage with everything they had: ketchup, mustard, relish, onions.

"Everything on a hot dog," he said. "I thought so."

"You guessed it on the first day." When Yolanda completed her dressing, she looked up at him to find a blank expression. "What's up?"

Samuel shook his head, his mouth in a thin line as he stared at her plate. "Nothing. I'm gonna get a drink," he said, backing away from the table.

"I'll see you by the bonfire?" Yolanda asked.

But he disappeared before answering, leaving her bewildered. *What was his problem?*

Yolanda grabbed a napkin and considered following him to the next table, but didn't get the chance when Julia pulled on her arm. "We're sitting over here," she said, quickly ushering Yolanda towards the bonfire. "I'm glad I didn't have to tell you not to get the potato salad."

Yolanda laughed. "I don't eat everybody's potato salad. What's wrong with this one?"

"Ugh," Julia grimaced. "It's got Craisens and pecans. I've never heard of such a thing."

"Has anyone broken out the guitar yet?" Yolanda asked as she checked out the circle of faculty members around the fire.

"Not yet," her friend giggled as she sat beside Brenda and Sarah, who were already starting with s'mores. "I saw you talking to Sam... what was that about?"

"Just business," Yolanda said, taking the first bite of her sausage.

"Risky business?"

As she chewed, her glance darted to Julia. Her grin was as wide as it was obnoxious. Yolanda swallowed before replying, "Nothing risky about syllabus talk. What about you and Pete?"

Julia's voice dropped to a whisper. "We're planning to meet up at the boathouse tonight."

Yolanda let out a small gasp. "To do what?"

Her friend rolled her eyes. "What do you think?"

Yolanda gave her an appraising nod. "Okay, Jules. Gettin' it in at summer camp."

"Everyone gather 'round," Craig called out. "I've got an announcement."

Yolanda and Julia both stifled their groans as Craig stood beside the fire. If it was another TB Activity, she would have to sit it out. She was officially done with team-building. The punch-drunk faces of her colleagues around the fire seemed to agree with her.

"I just want to thank you all for participating in the first-annual Getting Back to Humanities team-building retreat. Working with you all, on behalf of our students, brings me so much joy. And to see you work with one another this week, has been quite… entertaining." Yolanda couldn't help but laugh along with her colleagues. Entertaining, indeed. "Of course, none of this could have happened without the tireless efforts of Joanne Stuber. Come on up here Jo!"

They applauded and whistled as Joanne stood and walked to Craig. She nervously smoothed down her maroon Franklin University t-shirt and waved at the crowd. "It was nothing," she demurred.

"Not nothing," Craig corrected. "You are the backbone of the Humanities, Joanne, and I don't know if I could keep my head screwed on my shoulders if you weren't around." It could have been the heat of the fire or Craig's praise, but Joanne's face turned bright red. "That's why I want to give you tonight's last prize: a gift-card to Target, for $100."

Everyone cheered as Joanna flapped her hands in excitement. "Oh Craig," she flustered as she plucked the card from his hands, "oh, this is too much. My goodness, you shouldn't have. This is just—oh, Craig, really…"

Yolanda and Julia exchanged a grin. "They are the cutest," Julia whispered.

"Well, I know how much you like Target," Craig explained as his face also went red. "It's just a little something to show how much we appreciate you."

"Thank you so much," she said. They stood very close to one another, gazing into each other's eyes, both grinning ear-to-ear. For a moment, it was as if the rest of the faculty wasn't there.

But Craig soon cleared his throat and shoved his hands in

his pockets. "I know you had something you wanted to tell our Team Builders, Joanne."

"Yes!" she said abruptly. "Right. Every evening I asked you to write Daily Reflections, and I wanted to thank you all for doing that. I've been tracking your responses throughout the week, and well, there's a couple of TB Buddies who seemed to have come a long way since we started. Professors Watson and Morris, could you stand up for this?"

Yolanda froze mid-bite. "Mmh?"

Julia took her plate and urged her to stand up. When she did, she quickly chewed and searched the crowd for Samuel. He was standing directly behind her, beer in hand, and a tight smile.

"At the start of the week, I could tell you two were not having it," Joanne said with a laugh. "But around day three or four, something just changed. It was like a team-building light switch flipped. Could you tell the group what you guys learned?"

Yolanda gulped as Samuel took his place beside her. This was the most embarrassing thing that anyone had ever asked her to take part in. What in the hell was Joanne thinking? "I think…"

"—It was rough in the beginning, but I think some of these activities helped me break down some barriers I'd built up at Franklin. I learned that nothing bad is going to happen if I'm not perfect," he glanced at her. "Rather, Yolanda taught me."

"Right," she said in a shaky voice. "Sam's right. I look forward to learning from him—from all of you," she added quickly, "because I know I also have stuff to work on."

"And it's rare that team-building is strengthened by a bear encounter," Craig quipped, earning a laugh from the crowd.

"You never told us how that happened," said Gus Kelly, who quietly stoked the fire. "Were you scared of Old Smokey?"

"Of course," Yolanda said. "It was a giant bear."

Sam moved closer to her, placing his hand in the center of her back. The feeling of his hands on her was quickly becoming a familiar comfort. Every time he made the gesture, it put her at ease. "Old Smokey was a lone male, probably four hundred pounds. I'd say he was a seven-footer when he stood."

"Oh goodness, what did he sound like?" Joanna asked.

"He was fairly quiet; just a couple of grunts and huffs," Samuel answered expertly. "We knew not to run from him, but we had to scare him back to where he came from. In that moment, I think Yolanda kept her wits about her. She even had enough humor to quote a line from *Harry and The Hendersons*."

She frowned at him. "I did what?"

He looked down, trying not to laugh, his fingers pressing against her back. "You don't remember?"

Yolanda shook her head. Most of those terrifying moments were now a blur.

"I believe you shouted: 'can't you see we don't want you?' I think you shamed the bear into retreating."

Yolanda covered her face with her hand. "Thank you for that reminder..."

"How did you really scare it away?" Brenda asked.

"Sam suggested we make ourselves bigger and shout it down. Apparently we looked too wild for it to eat us."

"Now that's TB," Chris called out. "I would have tried to run faster than Peter."

"We don't have a special prize for you two," Craig said. "But it needs to be said that you took the TB Buddy challenge seriously and I applaud you both."

As the group clapped for them, Yolanda felt Samuel's hand slide up and down her back before dropping to his side. "I'm grateful for Rabbit Cabin to be out of commission," Yolanda said. "Or else I wouldn't have learned so much about Sam."

"Funny you say that," Gus piped up. "I forgot to tell y'all I fixed the bathroom in Rabbit Cabin two days ago. If you need a break from each other, you're welcome to it."

The silence that fell over the campfire made Yolanda blush. Were people looking to them to say something about their sleeping arrangements? She cast a nervous glance at Samuel. "I, uh... I mean, that's up to you."

To his credit, he didn't appear nervous. Instead, he flashed her a wide smile before wrapping his arm around her shoulder. "I think I'll stay with my TB Buddy, Gus. I'm already in charge of spider removal in Fox Cabin."

"Suit yourself," Gus said with a shrug.

When they sat down, everyone returned to their fireside chatter. "What was that?" Yolanda asked him.

"Spider removal is my job, right?"

"You're not bothered that people might assume stuff about us?" she asked in a quiet voice.

"For a moment, I was," he admitted as he stared into the fire. Bright flames played with the shadows of his face and made his green eyes glitter. When he licked his lips and rested his strong forearms on his knees, Yolanda's mouth went dry. When she thought he was her nemesis, she couldn't stand how handsome he was. Now, she wondered when they could sneak away for the next make-out session.

"And now?" she asked cautiously.

When he met her gaze, she almost gasped. His smiling eyes roved over her face before landing on her lips. They seemed to darken as he stared at her mouth. "I can worry about the gossip in Bear Cabin... or I can think about more entertaining things. What do you think I should devote my energy to?"

"You know me, I live to entertain…" Yolanda bit her lip. "You're not mad about that, are you?"

"I was nervous," he said. "But I know you didn't mean any harm."

"I didn't say anything that would embarrass you," she blurted. "Just that you were a really good kisser."

Samuel's surprised laughter lightened her heart. "That's all?"

"Nothing else," she promised. "I swear."

He shook his head and patted her knee. "I'm going back to the cabin. I feel like watching some *House* and waiting on you."

Yolanda's heart raced in anticipation. Waiting on her? She looked around the fire to see people enjoying themselves. Julia was eating the rest of her hot dog while chatting with Sarah and Brenda. No one would notice if they left tonight's festivities. She nodded. "Okay."

Samuel stood and walked away, leaving her with her jittery feelings. Yolanda sat there for a few minutes, half-listening to the women beside her and staring at the fire before her.

"You should go after him," Julia said in a soft voice.

"I was planning on it," she replied. "I was just giving him a head start."

Julia wrapped an arm around her shoulders and pulled her close. "What was it you said on the first day? You were going to shove me off a cliff like a jealous ex-husband?"

Yolanda chuckled. "Something to that effect."

"My, my, how the tables have turned…"

Chapter Twelve

Once the kitchen staff began serving alcohol, the Humanities College became a full-on bacchanalia, making it easier for Yolanda to slip away unnoticed. Her walk back to Fox Cabin was slow, but her thoughts bounced wildly through her mind as she considered her relationship with Samuel Morris.

About five days ago, she called him a nemesis.

Tonight, she was going to fuck him silly in a cabin.

When she made it to the front door, Yolanda had to collect herself. She smoothed her t-shirt down and checked her back-pocket for the condom she hid earlier that morning. When she left him in Fox Cabin, she'd already made plans for tonight. She just hoped he was down to play. "Okay, girl," she whispered to herself. "You've got this."

When she opened the door, she found a shirtless Samuel laying in bed. He looked up with a beaming smile. "Hey."

The unexpected sight made her fall against the door-frame and stare. He had no right to look that sexy in khaki shorts slung low on his hips. His dark brown hair flopped over his wire-framed glasses as he grinned at her. Yolanda's heart kicked into a full gallop. Whatever sexy plan she thought she'd execute died on the doorstep as she struggled to say something cuter than "hey." She took a deep breath and fumbled to close the door. "You weren't waiting long, were you?"

Samuel closed the laptop and shook his head. "Not long at all."

"That's good," she said, slipping her shoes off. "I'm just gonna go to the bathroom real quick…" She escaped before he could reply. In the bathroom, she flicked on the light and shut the door before checking herself in the mirror. There was no reason to be as nervous as she was, but Yolanda knew this wasn't light-fingering after a near bear attack. This was premeditated fucking. And she wasn't ready. She splashed cold water on her face because she'd seen people do it in movies. It did not help.

As she searched the bathroom for an answer to her nerves, her eyes landed on her beauty products. After several days of using them, Samuel was still organizing her things. Even this morning, she hadn't remembered to straighten her mess. She put on lotion, spritzed herself with perfume, and used both tubs of edge control and styling gel. He stacked them like toy blocks, large to small. His consideration made her smile. He probably couldn't help himself, but Yolanda could have done a better job of sharing space with another person. It was selfish of her to leave such a mess and expect him to contend with it.

Amid the order, Yolanda got an idea.

"Sam? Can you come here?" she asked as she opened the door.

She heard him rise from his bed. "Are you okay?" he asked. "Is there another spider?"

"No, not that."

He stood in the doorway, his gaze flitting from her to the bathtub. "What's wrong?"

"Come here."

Samuel's eyes narrowed before taking a hesitant step inside. He stood behind her, watching her amused expression through the mirror's reflection. "What's so funny?"

Yolanda teethed her bottom lip as her grin widened. "I want you to do something for me."

He didn't reply, but a dark brow raised above his glasses.

"Knock that stack of jars over," she said, pointing to her beauty products.

His eyes followed her gesture and his mouth twisted. "Why would I do that?"

"Because it's fun to make a mess." His silence told her he was seriously considering it. He stared at what he had meticulously organized and swallowed. "I can get you started..." Yolanda swatted at the small jar of edge-control, sending it flying into the sink. They watched it tumbled and skittered to a standstill.

Samuel met her gaze in the mirror and rolled his eyes. "What is this supposed to do?"

"Will it relax you if I promise to clean it up after we're finished?"

"We're finished?"

She pulled the condom out of her back-pocket and laid it on the counter. "After we're finished," she said, nodding to it.

Samuel struggled not to smile. "You're incorrigible."

Perhaps it was working? She noticed how close he stood behind her and waited for him to close the distance, for him to press himself flush against her back. Yolanda raised her chin as a challenge. "Knock it over, Sam."

He bit back his grin as he stepped closer. "You won't be satisfied until I do it?"

"I won't," she said, shaking her head. "This is a part of your training."

Samuel sighed. "Fine…" He slowly lifted his hand to the nearest tower of body butter, coconut oil, and leave-in conditioner. "Knock it over?"

"Please," she whispered. "Destroy it."

His gaze darted back to her's before he gently pushed the products to the floor. The loud clatter made her giggle. "Happy?"

"More!"

Like a petulant cat, Samuel batted another tower that included some of his things. A bottle of aftershave and toner landed in the sink, a hairbrush hit the floor, combs and face wash spilled across the counter. Yolanda cheered while he chuckled against her shoulder. "Good enough?"

"Brilliant," she said. "Now take a deep breath."

Samuel closed his eyes and inhaled through his nose. When he exhaled, his hands landed on her hips. "How did you know that would make me feel better?" he asked in a low voice. With his eyes still on hers, he dipped his head to kiss her neck.

The sensation of his soft lips pressed against the hollow of her neck melted her bones and made her lean into his muscular chest. "When we get back to the city, I'm taking you to one of those rage rooms," she breathed, "so you can break shit and let loose some of this tension."

He chuckled against her skin, sending vibrations to the center of her chest. "I think you and I can find an easier way to do that, Yolanda." His hands skimmed down her thighs as he pressed himself against her back. Their eyes locked in the mirror as she *felt* just how tense he really was… She gripped the edge of the counter, holding still while he caressed her body. "Do you want to make a mess with me?"

His simple question stole her breath. All she could do was

nod.

He replied by closing his teeth around her earlobe and growling in her ear. "It shocks me how badly I want you, Yolanda. I now lie awake at night, desperate to touch you, to run my hands along your body like this." His hands snaked up her torso until they reached her breasts. He squeezed the swells beneath her t-shirt and sighed. "I feel like a wild man whenever I'm near you."

His reckless words, coupled with his strong hands, dampened her panties and made her stomach clench. She could barely keep track of where he touched her, she only knew pleasurable sensations emanating from vague points on her body. Her breasts, heavy and aching, felt like putty in his hands. The kisses at her neck sent a shiver down her back as his hot breath fanned against her cool skin. She lolled her head to the side and closed her eyes. "Get wild, Sam," she said, reaching down to undo her shorts.

His hand shot down, capturing her own. "No," he said in a stern voice. "I'll do it."

When she opened her eyes, Samuel's glittering green gaze stared back at her. With her heart caught in her throat, she croaked, "Yeah?"

"Let me have a little control before I lose it all."

As far as she could tell, he was already on the edge. His hair was ruffled and his glasses were fogged up. "Go ahead."

In the reflection, she watched him slowly unbutton her shorts before pushing them over the curve of her ass. She stepped out of them and nudged them away with her toe. Samuel took less care getting out of his own pants, which he had kicked somewhere outside of the bathroom. Yolanda tried to turn to see his black boxer-briefs, but he stopped her. "Eyes front, honey."

Her mouth fell open. "Are you bossing me around?"

He smirked. "Let me lead this activity," he said, nodding to the mirror. "I want you to watch the show from there. I want you to see how much I need you." He rocked his hips against her body, rubbing his hot erection along the crease of her cheeks. "I want you to *feel* how much I need you."

She gasped at his dirty talk, wondering how long he'd wanted to speak to her like this. But Samuel had more surprises in store. She nearly fell apart when he licked his fingers before dipping them into the front of her panties. Like yesterday, he understood where he needed to touch, how much pressure to apply, and for how long. His long dexterous fingers plucked at her like a concert violinist until her knees buckled under her weight. "You didn't need to do that," she panted as she held on to the counter. She could have sworn she was already wet enough...

He smiled from over her shoulder. "I know," he said, dipping two fingers inside of her, stroking her wetness. "But I really wanted to."

Just outside of their cabin, she heard the echoes of the bonfire party. It reminded her how alone they were, yet how close they were to their colleagues. Yolanda felt a carnal thrill as she listened to distant laughter while watching Samuel's brow furrow in concentration. "Please," she panted.

His fingers and thumb worked together expertly, rubbing inside and out. She doubled over and he followed, holding her close and panting in her ear. Yolanda could no longer keep track of the movements, she only knew raw lust clawing through her body like a ravenous animal. She chased the feeling blindly, writhing against Samuel's insistent hand. Her breath came in

133

ragged gasps until the dam broke and she spilled into an abyss, a bright expanse of spasms and waves that swept over her until her body weakened and her cries became groans.

As quick as she came, Yolanda was greedy for more pleasure. It wasn't enough to be wrapped in Samuel's tight embrace, his hand still cupping her. She stared at herself in the mirror and was almost embarrassed by what she saw. The outlines of her nipples poked through her t-shirt as his strong arm crossed her belly. Her thighs spread scandalously to accommodate his hand. Her eyes glazed over from an orgasm… They were wild *together*.

"That was wonderful," she whispered to his reflection.

Samuel turned her to face him, tilted her head back, and kissed her roughly. She groaned against his mouth as he crushed her to him. His lips were hard, his tongue searching, burning her with a renewed hunger that made her hot all over again. While succumbing to his devouring kiss, Yolanda shimmied out of her underwear and clumsily propped herself on the counter. Samuel blindly fumbled with the condom, unwrapping it while she pulled him between her thighs. After a few more seconds, he finally pulled away to breathe and sheathe himself.

Yolanda also took that respite to catch her breath and, more importantly, to sneak a glance at his dick. Of course, it looked just as impressive as it felt pressed against her ass: thick and hard. She delighted in the way he gripped himself, wishing he was using her hands instead. Tomorrow, she would get her chance to investigate further… For now, she concentrated on the way he leveled the bulbous tip at her opening. Samuel glanced at her for confirmation. "Would you like me to continue?"

"If you don't, I'll be very disappointed," she chuckled as she slipped her shirt over her head and undid her bra.

"I don't want to disappoint," he said. "You might want to hold on, honey."

She didn't have to be told twice.

Yolanda held on to his shoulder and the counter as she widened her thighs. When he filled her, she inhaled sharply and arched against his chest. "Oooh, okay..." she breathed. "Yeeeesss..."

"That's okay?" he grunted.

More than *okay*. She was plenty primed for this moment and accepted him readily. Every inch he pushed into her felt like a gift. She nodded vigorously. "Definitely." Her pussy clenched around him and waited for his strokes.

"You feel amazing," he said through gritted teeth. "Everything about you... is so soft and beautiful." She shivered in anticipation as his intense gaze searched her entire body with reverence. Yolanda couldn't remember a time when she felt so treasured. He slowly withdrew before pushing back into her, pushing all rational thoughts right out of her head. Every stroke was long and hard enough for her to forget her name and where she was being fucked.

Samuel's hands didn't know where they wanted to be. One minute, they were on her breasts massaging and caressing; the next minute, his fingers were dug into her hair, pulling her close for another devastating kiss. While he kissed and petted her, she focused on keeping pace with his strokes, which started slow but soon picked up steam. She chased her second orgasm on top of the bathroom counter, legs wrapped around Samuel's hips. "Oh god, Sam..."

"Are you close?" he asked.

Yolanda could barely get the word out. She simply nodded and hugged him closer.

He gripped her thigh, fingers digging into her plump flesh. "I want to hear it, Yolanda," he said with a harsh breath. "Tell me."

His demanding tone made her pussy even wetter. "I'm close," she squeaked.

"Let me see you touch yourself," he whispered in her ear.

If Samuel didn't shut up, he was going to make her slippery enough to slide right off the counter. Still, she freed one hand to touch her sensitive clit; her fingertips brushed against his dick as it drove in and out of her. The sound of their pants and moans was the erotic symphony she stroked herself to. "I'm going to come," she whispered, on the verge of tears.

"Fuck…" he said with a hitched breath, "…yes. Goddamn, me too. You feel like a dream, Yolanda." He buried his face into the crook of her neck and groaned. "Oh, fuck…"

For the second time that evening, Yolanda pitched forward, flailing for something to hold her steady while an orgasm rippled through every fiber of her being. She clutched Samuel's broad shoulders tightly as she rode through multiple waves of dizzying pleasure, cresting and peaking until her thighs trembled around him. In her sex-haze, she vaguely noticed the increased speed against her fluttering walls, but barely had the energy to stay with him. She just held on to dear life while he climaxed.

Samuel came just like she assumed he would, in a low panting groan that became a pained growl. Truly wild. They rode the wave together, clutching one another until they could come down. She felt his body shake and shudder as he spent himself and muttered curses against her neck. This was the one time when Yolanda could hear Samuel's filthy, desperate language.

He was a babbling, incoherent mess in her arms, and she was happy to hold him up as he sank against her.

"Yolanda," he said after a long pause.

"Sam?"

"Can we keep doing that?"

She rubbed his sweat-slicked skin and sighed contently. "Yes, please."

He pulled out of her and disposed of his condom in quick order. "Can I take you to bed?" he asked.

His politeness made her giggle. "Yes, please."

Samuel hitched her thighs around his waist and carried her to the other part of the cabin before gently laying her in his bed. From her vantage point, she could fully appreciate his nudity. Yolanda unabashedly admired his long lean frame with muscular pecs and stacked abs descending down his torso. And she especially loved the light smattering of dark chest hair that thinned into a slender line down the center of his belly...

"Pinch me," Yolanda said.

Samuel cocked an eyebrow. "Why would I do that?"

"Because I'm having such a sexy time with the man who I thought was my nemesis. I feel like a fool, and I regret not flirting with you a year ago. Pinch me."

He eyed her cautiously while giving her a soft pinch on her forearm. "Will that do?"

Yolanda sighed, "I'm sorry for being so hard-headed, Sam. I'm sorry for not getting to know you until now."

His face softened. "I kinda like how hard-headed you are. And getting to know you has been lovely, much better than the Assessment Committee."

She believed him.

Except tomorrow, things might change. He might get on that

bus and become another person. They might both go back to being enemies when they got to Chicago. Yolanda wanted to keep things the way they were in this moment. As she held on to Samuel, her mind drifted past him. To a place where they hung out on separate sides of their buildings, not interacting until they absolutely had to.

"Stop thinking," Samuel said in a stern voice.

He brought her back to the present. "I like you very much, Sam. Chicago won't change that, will it?"

"I like *you* very much. I want to like you even more in Chicago," Samuel said, sinking down beside her. "The only thing that will change is your smoke detector. I plan on repairing it when I visit because I'm now very concerned about your safety."

She laughed as she snuggled beside him. "You make me sound like a mess!"

"I like your mess," he said, kissing her shoulder.

"You lie."

"Some messes are nice," he insisted.

"They're better with you," she whispered.

Samuel wrapped his arms around her middle and held her close. "You have me."

Yolanda leaned into him and looked up into his gorgeous forest-green eyes and sighed. With his powerful arms surrounding her, she felt safe enough to say: "And you have me too, Sam."

Epilogue

Yolanda had kept her eyes open.

And she even took notes.

Ted Hanover, the Writing Center director, was wrapping up his grant-writing workshop when she realized that she had learned quite a bit. Samuel sat beside her and took copious notes in a small legal pad while three other professors, from the Sciences, followed along.

On the fourth week of fall semester classes, Yolanda made good on her promise to attend a workshop. Samuel had sent her the link one evening while they laid in his bed. He waited until she confirmed attendance before going down on her. She would have agreed to anything to get his face between her thighs. She tried to sulk over his dirty trick, but after one swipe of his tongue, Yolanda quickly caved under the pleasure.

"Anyway, if you need any reminders, you can find my PowerPoint on the writing center website, along with some other helpful resources to get you started," Ted said as he turned off the projector and packed up his things.

The workday was over for many of the people in the room. And as they shuffled out, leaving Yolanda and Sam alone, she looked up to find him staring at her. "What?" she asked, breaking the silence in the small meeting room.

His smile crinkled the corners of his eyes. He glanced at her notes before returning to her face. "You didn't mind the workshop?"

Yolanda shook her head. "Ted is a great teacher. I'll definitely come back."

Samuel bumped her shoulder playfully. "And in the interim, maybe I can teach you other things?"

Had anyone seen the two of them together, they would have found them to be an odd pair. Yolanda in her jeans and Ziggy Stardust t-shirt; Samuel in his starched white button down and charcoal slacks. He was "looser" these days, which meant he rolled his sleeves to the elbows and skipped the necktie. "Mmh... what lessons would you have in mind?" she asked, leaning forward and propping her chin on her fist.

Samuel pulled his glasses from his face and tucked them in his shirt pocket. She instantly missed them. His glasses made him even cuter. "We still need to work on your citation, Yolanda. The world doesn't revolve around MLA, you know."

Her lips curled into a sly smile. "Your place or mine?"

"Yours is fine," he purred, leaning closer until his face nuzzled her curls. She heard him inhale deeply before whispering. "Do you have pancake fixings for the morning?"

"I do."

Yolanda's eyes drifted closed as she fell into his gravitational pull. The windowless room in the writing center offered them a small measure of privacy. If she could steal a kiss from him on campus, that would be a thrilling new step in their relationship.

Relationship....

The word made her heart light with hope and anticipation for the future. When she imagined a future with Samuel, it felt like this: him nuzzled against her neck, making plans in between classes, spending evenings alternating between their two apartments. Those images made her smile. Samuel made her happy.

He pulled back slightly until they were nearly nose-to-nose. "What's on your mind, Professor Watson?"

"Us," she whispered. "I like us a lot."

Samuel beamed. "You know, for a literature professor, that wasn't very eloquent... but I like us a lot, too. I also like the way you smile, the way you laugh with your entire body." He pressed a soft kiss against the pulse of her neck. When she sighed, he kissed her again. "I like that sound, too."

Yolanda raised a hand to his chest. "Let me try again. You are such a lovely man, and I enjoy learning about you. Your laugh is my favorite sound, but I love your smile the most."

He chuckled darkly. The sound vibrated against her neck, sending a shiver of pleasure down to her belly. "I'll try to give it to you whenever I can." He sat up and looked her in the eye. "When I have tunnel-vision, you think of all the possibilities. That makes me smile."

Yolanda fingered the small patch of skin revealed by his open collar. "Thank you, Sam."

"Now, are you ready to head home?"

She nodded. "Episode of *House* tonight?"

"Maybe we can catch the new episode of *The Real Housewives of...* whatever." Samuel stood and gathered his things. "We have to find out what happened at whoever's fashion party."

Yolanda followed him, taking him by the hand. Once they were in the hallway of Williamson Hall, he squeezed her hand and brought her close to his side. She looked up at him and grinned. His back was as straight as an arrow and his strong chin pointed forward. Samuel was going to stay Samuel, and she was ready to accept him as he was: rigid work-ethic, neat, and tidy. To his credit, he accepted her quirky chaos, distracted rambling, and messy mind.

As they headed towards the exit, Yolanda leaned back to check out Samuel's khaki-covered butt. She really, *really* liked her tight-ass Virgo.

About the Author

Charish Reid is a fan of sexy books and disaster films. When she's not grading papers or prepping lessons for college freshmen, she enjoys writing romances that celebrate quirky Black women who deserve HEAs. Charish currently lives in Sweden, with her husband, avoiding most forms of exercise.

You can connect with me on:

- https://charishreid.com
- https://twitter.com/AuthorCharish
- https://www.facebook.com/CharishReidAuthor
- https://www.instagram.com/charishreidauthor

Also by Charish Reid

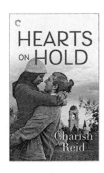

Hearts on Hold

What happens in the stacks stays in the stacks...

Professor Victoria Reese knows an uphill battle when she sees one. Convincing her narrow-minded colleagues at the elite Pembroke University to back a partnership with the local library is a fight she saw coming and already has a plan for. What she didn't see coming? The wildly hot librarian who makes it clear books aren't the only thing he'd like to handle.

When a tightly wound, sexy-as-hell professor proposes a partnership between his library and her university, children's department head John Donovan is all for it. He knows his tattoos and easygoing attitude aren't quite what she expected, but the unmistakable heat between them is difficult to resist.

And then there's the intriguing late fee on her record. *For the Duke's Convenience...* A late fee and a sexy romance novel? There's more to Dr. Reese than she's letting on.

John might like to tease her about her late fee, but when he teases her in other ways, Victoria is helpless to resist. Mixing business with pleasure—and oh, it *is* pleasure—always comes with risks, but maybe a little casual fun between the sheets is just what Victoria needs.

The Write Escape
Take one heartbroken Chicago girl

Literary editor Antonia Harper had it all—the career, the man, the future. That was then. Now Antonia is jobless, alone and at a crossroads. What better time to travel the world? A solo honeymoon on the Emerald Isle will be like hitting the reset button. No distractions, no drama.

Add some luck o' the Irish

Aiden Byrnes may be a literature professor, but words fail him when he meets the woman staying in the cottage next door. Tully Cross is meant to be a sleepy little village, and he's meant to be on a working holiday—not a vacation, and most definitely not with his beautiful neighbor.

And you get some mighty good *craic*

They say laughter is the best medicine—and as it turns out, superhot sex isn't so bad either. Antonia and Aiden's spark quickly grows into what could be something special, if they're willing to take the leap. Ending up an ocean apart is unthinkable, and when real life comes calling, there's no ignoring that leap anymore…

Made in the USA
Middletown, DE
17 June 2021